"Unca Joel is walking with me. You can come?" little Caleb asked Beth.

"No, but thank you for the offer. I need to be heading home. I've got some things to do," Beth replied.

"Go ahead, walk with us," Joel invited. "I'll use the time to ask you out again and to thank you for saving my life."

"I didn't save your life. You'd have regained consciousness and driven yourself to the hospital."

"No, I wouldn't have. I needed you."

"Well, you've said thank-you already. That's enough." She checked her watch. "I need to be going."

"You're right," Joel jumped in. "Going out with me? Tonight? Dinner?"

"Joel, you'll be here for a few months and then you'll leave. You've always been really good at leaving people behind," Beth said, tussling Caleb's hair and heading for her car.

"You take every opportunity to throw that in my face. Maybe I never knew they cared."

It was too late. She was out of hearing range.

Caleb tugged on Joel's pant leg. "I care."

Books by Pamela Tracy

Love Inspired

Daddy for Keeps
Once Upon a Cowboy

Love Inspired Suspense

Pursuit of Justice
The Price of Redemption
Broken Lullaby
Fugitive Family
Clandestine Cover-Up

PAMELA TRACY

is an award-winning author who lives with her husband (he claims to be the inspiration for most of her heroes) and son (he claims to be the interference for most of her writing time). She started writing at a very young age (a series of romances, all with David Cassidy as the hero. Sometimes Bobby Sherman would interfere). Then, while earning a BA in journalism at Texas Tech University in Lubbock, Texas, she picked up the pen again (this time, it was an electric typewriter on which she wrote a very bad science-fiction novel).

First published in 1999, Pamela is a winner of the American Christian Fiction Writer's Book of the Year award and has been a RITA® Award finalist. Readers can write to her at www.pamelakayetracy.com or c/o Love Inspired Books, 233 Broadway, Suite 1001, New York, NY 01279. You can find out more about Pamela by visiting her blog, Craftie Ladies of Suspense, at www.ladiesofsuspense.blogspot.com.

Once Upon a Cowboy

Pamela Tracy

*Love*Inspired

Recycling programs
for this product may
not exist in your area.

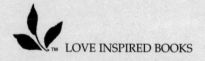

LOVE INSPIRED BOOKS

ISBN-13: 978-0-373-81567-8

ONCE UPON A COWBOY

www.LoveInspiredBooks.com

Printed in U.S.A.

But while he was still a long way off, his father saw him and was filled with compassion for him; he ran to his son, threw his arms around him and kissed him.
—*Luke* 15:20

To those returning and those who never strayed: both take courage. Also, to the mothers, fathers, sisters, and brothers who welcome the wanderers home.

Chapter One

A memory knocked.

Before Beth Armstrong had time to even think about opening the door to the past, she slammed on her brakes, hard. Her wheels slid and the car went sideways until she finally came to an abrupt stop facing the royal blue truck that looked hauntingly familiar.

The truck wasn't going anywhere. Not after the power skid that took it off-road, bouncing over an irrigation ditch and plowing into the McClanahans' fence.

Help me, Lord, and please let whoever is in there be all right. Don't let this be a fatality.

She pushed open her car's door and—with only the moon to witness her flight—managed to make it through the grass, then down and up the irrigation ditch. She climbed clumsily over one of the broken fence posts using the truck to steady herself.

The vehicle was caught in mangled barbed wire

and still warm to the touch. The smell of gas and exhaust warred with the strong aroma of the McClanahans' hay field. She balanced on the shattered fence, trying to get the courage to move forward and wishing she had more than the glow from her headlights combined with the truck's taillights to assist her. As if answering her prayer, the truck's driver's side door opened, and the light from the inside dome gave her all the illumination she needed.

The memory stopped knocking. Just one look at what lay in the truck's bed—a gear bag and bull rope—opened the door to the past and let the memory in.

Joel McCreedy.

The prodigal son.

It had been more than eight years since he'd been the focus of her girlhood fantasies.

He didn't look like a fantasy now. He slouched forward against the steering wheel, his face turned her way. His eyes were closed, and a trickle of blood ran from a cut just above his left eye. She closed her eyes. *Blood. Not good.*

Opening her eyes, she reached in and gently touched his shoulder. "Joel, are you awake? Are you okay?" Her voice sounded loud in the silence of the moment. He didn't move at all. She looked at his chest to make sure it moved up and down. It did. He was still alive.

"Joel!"

He moaned, didn't open his eyes and then slumped

forward. This time, his chest hit the horn. Beth nearly toppled over thanks to her precarious perch, before shouting again, this time over the noise, "Joel!"

Well, okay, she could holler Joel's name until the cows came home for all the good it would do. Not that he'd be able to hear her over the blare of his horn. Carefully, she nudged him back so he wasn't pushed against the steering wheel. Nothing changed, not the expression on his face or the stillness of his body.

Roanoke had one ambulance, and she could get him to town faster than it could get here, most likely. "Joel, you might need to help a bit here."

His eyelids fluttered, and he grunted. She took both hands and shoved with all her strength. As he slowly adjusted to the passenger side, papers, folders and what looked like a Bible fell to the floorboard. "You weigh a ton, Joel," she muttered.

"And that's just my aching head," he moaned.

Good, at least he was conscious and somewhat lucid. When he was finally settled on the passenger side, she let out her breath. She got behind the wheel and tried closing the door—no such luck—so she buckled her seat belt and put his truck in Reverse.

One thing about old, old trucks. They were made of pure steel. Backing up, Beth managed to destroy a bit more of the McClanahans' fence. She bounced over the irrigation ditch and skidded only a bit on the dirt road as she aimed for traction and headed into town, stopping just long enough to turn off her own car's headlights and grab her purse, before hurrying back to Joel's truck.

He hadn't moved.

With one hand clutching the door closed and the other clasped tight on the steering wheel, she made it maybe half a mile before Joel finally stirred again and turned to look at her. In the shadows, she couldn't see his eyes, but she knew they were a deep brown and full of hurt.

She had a million questions and not all of them had to do with his health. Joel McCreedy, the prodigal son, back in Roanoke, Iowa. He must have just arrived, because if he'd been here a day or two, she'd have known.

She braced herself and let the driver's side door swing open. Then, she pulled her cell phone from her pocket and hit the zero. She should have done that first thing. After a moment, an operator came on and Beth asked for hospital emergency. Once she'd warned them about what to expect, she hung up and tossed her cell phone on the dash. It promptly slid to the ground. Forcing the door to close again and holding it tightly, she again looked at the man slumped next to her, suddenly aware of the feel of his weight leaning against her right arm.

His forehead hadn't been hot, but his body was. She could feel it through her sleeve. His blue T-shirt was tight against a rock hard chest. Jeans covered legs so long they reached the passenger side door.

His eyes remained shut, but a tiny bit of color had returned to his face. The trickle of blood started to drip off his chin and onto his shirt.

As if to remind her not to look there, not to dwell on the blood, the truck hit a bump, and Beth's head almost hit the roof.

For the next half hour, until lights shimmered in the distance and the town came into view, Beth concentrated on keeping the driver's side door shut, listening to make sure Joel still breathed and making it to town. Easing up on the gas, Beth passed the convenience store and small motel beyond the Welcome to Roanoke, Iowa sign. The hospital was just a few blocks in. Joel finally twitched a little, shifting his weight away from her, but instead of feeling relief that he was finally giving her space, she felt loss.

Not what she needed.

Joel McCreedy was no longer the boy she remembered. But he was still the man most of the town wanted to forget.

In the scheme of things, a little blood and a wicked headache were the least of Joel McCreedy's problems.

Nothing was going as planned. This wasn't how he had imagined his homecoming. Even in his wildest nightmares—and after riding a good draw named Homeless a few weeks ago, he'd had some pretty wild ones—he'd not figured on being turned away

from his childhood home, wrecking his beloved truck
and then being escorted to the hospital by a gorgeous
female.

He was lucky she'd been on the deserted road that
late at night and was willing to stop.

"We almost there?" he asked, careful not to move
his head. Waves of pain were just one more unwelcome reminder of a lousy evening.

"Five minutes," she answered, not wasting words.
He liked that.

She obviously knew him, had called him by name,
and knew her way around Roanoke. If it didn't hurt
so much to talk, he'd ask her name. Instead, he concentrated on keeping his head still and gritting his
teeth every time she hit a bump.

"When did you get back, Joel?"

Joel closed his eyes. He'd made it to Solitaire Farm
sometime this evening. How long ago? Thirty minutes? An hour? Two? Did it matter?

"This evening," he finally answered. The sky had
already turned to night when his beloved, aged 1958
royal blue Ford truck idled in front of the sign reading Solitaire Farm. A home he'd turned his back on
almost a decade ago and that had now turned its back
on him.

No more questions followed. Maybe she figured
from his short answers that he wasn't up for conversation.

Truth was, he wasn't up for much of anything else,
either. He'd left New Mexico yesterday, pretty much

driving straight through. He'd caught a catnap or two at rest stops. Still, he'd had almost twenty-four hours of sitting in one position, trying to ignore the pain in his back and the pain in his heart.

Without the rodeo, where did he belong?

They reached the tiny Roanoke hospital. She managed to hit the curb as she pulled into the parking lot, and then skidded to a stop in front of the emergency room doors.

More medical bills, great.

There wasn't but five dollars in his pocket. He did, however, already have a folder full of medical expenses—with more to come—and a stack of unpaid credit card bills. The debt and his need for family were about to increase.

He'd waited too long and now instead of a hero's welcome and a bank account guaranteed to make his older brother sit up and take notice, Joel had his tail between his legs.

The legs that weren't strong enough to allow him to walk into the emergency room alone. Instead, he had to lean on a young woman whose name he couldn't recall and a hospital attendant he recognized from his high school graduating class.

Kyle Tuckee was the attendant's name. He'd been two years ahead of Joel and a second stringer for the football team. He seemed to move a lot faster now, sprinting from the emergency room door to Joel's truck.

Through the glass doors, Joel also recognized the

woman manning the front desk. She'd been a friend of his mother's. She raised an eyebrow at the sight of Joel, quickly recovered and hurried to assist. She opened a swinging door and soon Joel was escorted into a tiny room with a bed and chair.

"What happened? When did Joel get home?" Delores Peabody asked, helping him into the bed and reaching for a blood pressure cuff.

Joel closed his eyes. Nausea kept him from answering, but his hearing still worked.

"I don't know how long he's been back," his rescuer said. She really was quite beautiful, with blond hair just reaching her shoulders and a compact body. He was tempted to open his eyes again, just to get another look. Unfortunately, she wasn't done talking. "And he's not with me, not really, and please don't tell my mother that I'm the one who brought him here. I just happened to see him drive off the road."

Joel's interest was piqued, but before the women could say more the doctor came in. He asked the nurse a few questions and came over to stand next to Joel.

"How are you feeling?"

"Head hurts," was all Joel managed to say.

The young woman started in, and this time she didn't say anything about her mother, just got straight to the point. "He was driving east on Rural Route 7 and went off the road. He didn't slow down or anything. He hit the McClanahans' fence, I'd say maybe forty-five minutes ago, probably going about fifty.

When I got to him, he was pitched forward. He was unconscious then, but only for a moment, and he had a cut above his left eye, which kept bleeding. I figured I could get him here faster than the ambulance could get there. I scooted him over because I didn't think I could get him out of his truck and into my car. Will he be all right?"

"Are you family?" the doctor asked.

"No, more a friend of the family."

"Has family been contacted?"

Delores said, "I'll do that now." She left the room, and the younger woman followed.

Funny, throughout this whole mess, until tonight, Joel had been on his own. He'd already done the hospitalization route—for two days after he lost the ability to walk. Then he'd started physical therapy before running out of money.

He'd been alone but hadn't really felt alone.

Until now.

Beth had a total of four hours of sleep, thanks to Joel McCreedy and then the emergency room. It had been almost midnight by the time she had retrieved her car with the help of her oldest sister and roommate, and then finally made it home to their small house on Oak Street. She'd been too keyed up to even think about going to bed.

Bad move.

Roanoke Elementary would celebrate its hundred year anniversary this year. Just three weeks ago,

Beth had started her second year as its kindergarten teacher. Fridays were always rough, but today was one for the record book.

"Miss Armstrong," one of her girls said, "you already read us that page."

"Twice," another bright little girl spoke up.

"Keep reading," a little boy suggested.

Little Mitzi Gabor tapped Beth on the knee. "Maybe we could have free time?" she said in a hopeful whisper.

"Good idea," Beth whispered back.

Soon, she had a classroom full of kids playing cars, building towers, coloring and some even sitting at their desks with a book. Most of the kids who chose to read looked content. Matt McCreedy, frowning at an upside-down book, looked lonely.

As Beth headed for her own desk to do a little catch-up work, she wondered what he was really seeing.

Beth knew what she *wished* she wasn't seeing. Her mother, the school secretary, walking by the classroom, lips pursed, a half dozen times.

Since the three Armstrong girls hit puberty, their mother had had two purposes: educate the girls so they could be self-sufficient and/or keep the girls safe and marry them off to nice churchgoing doctors or lawyers or business owners. Patsy wasn't old-fashioned or a snob. She just wanted her daughters to graduate from college and/or be married to men who chose nice, safe, well-paying professions.

Two areas in which Mom felt her own life had suffered.

Beth's oldest sister, Linda, hadn't met either criteria: no college, no nice young man. Middle sister, Susan, had started college, but dropped out to get married and Mom didn't really approve of her husband's profession as a police officer.

Not a *safe* career.

Her mother's dreams settled like a yoke across Beth's shoulders. Attending teachers college hadn't been a choice, it had been an order. To save money, Beth had managed to graduate in three years instead of four. And right now, her mother was championing the new youth minister at their church. Being a youth minister wasn't a well-paying job, but Nathan Fisher was also a physical therapist.

Beth set most of the class to cleaning up their seat area. Then, row by row, she called them by her desk where the mailboxes were. With the exception of Matt, all did her bidding.

He'd been even more lethargic than usual today. No doubt she could blame some of it on his uncle Joel and a late-night call from the hospital. Quite a lot for a five-year-old to handle.

No tiny bits of paper were on the floor by his desk. He'd barely started his cutting project. As for crayons, he had only used three—a brown, a black and a red—and they were stored in his crayon box. The upside-down book was already placed neatly in his desk. His lunch box, she knew, contained a peanut butter sandwich with three small bite marks.

That was all she could convince him to eat.

"Come on, Matt. You have a few papers to take home."

He shrugged. This wasn't what Mandy would have wanted.

Which was why Beth had headed to Solitaire Farm last night. She'd been mad, and although she wasn't one to act on impulse, when Jared hadn't shown up for his parent-teacher conference time, she'd taken it personally.

So at seven-thirty, after she'd finally gotten her classroom back in order and prepped for the following day, she'd headed for Solitaire Farm and Matt McCreedy's father.

After a long day on the farm, Jared hadn't been in the mood to hear what she had to say. He'd promised to reschedule. Thanked her for caring enough to make a home visit. Then, politely walked her to her car.

She and Linda had been his late wife's best friends. Mandy had been in Linda's class, but had always identified with the youngest Armstrong, treating her as a favorite kid sister and then an adult best friend. For nine years, Solitaire Farm had been a second home. That Mandy's sons were suffering broke Beth's heart.

"Matt, I need you to get your backpack."

"Anything I can do to help?"

Beth swallowed. Joel was standing in her classroom doorway and didn't look like he'd been in an automobile accident at all.

She blurted the first words that came to mind. "What are you doing here?"

He grinned, and eight years of maturity completely deserted her in one heart-melting moment—taking her right back to her schoolgirl crush.

"I'm feeling much better," he said. "Just a mild concussion. Thanks for asking. I'm lucky you were around to help. As for what I'm doing here, I needed to get my truck in for service. Without it, I either walk or hitch rides. I told Billy I'd meet him here at three."

"Here, as in my classroom?" The words came out more accusing than she meant them to be. But she didn't need any more questions from fellow teachers, not about Joel. And she certainly didn't need her mother to come marching down the hallway, all pursed lips and disapproving. Plus, she was a bit concerned about the look on Matt's face. The boy was staring at his uncle half in awe and half in terror.

"I also need to return this." He pulled her cell phone from his back jeans pocket.

"Miss Armstrong, Mitzi put trash on my floor," came a small, accusing voice.

Sure enough, little Mitzi, instead of walking all the way to the classroom trash can, had dumped her paper, her broken crayons and her half-eaten chicken finger by another student's desk.

A third student added to the fray, "Teacher, I gotta go…"

Joel smiled and laid the phone on a bookcase by the door. "I'll let you get back to work. Maybe you'll let me take you out for dinner some night as a proper thank-you."

"I don't think so," Beth said, giving Mitzi a look that sent her scurrying to clean up her mess *again*. She tried the same look on Joel, but it only made his grin widen before he left her classroom.

What really amazed Beth was how easily he waltzed into and out of the elementary school, without the tiniest hint of guilt. Now, her mother would do more than just walk by Beth's door with her lips pursed. Now, the other teachers and some of the parents wouldn't start with the polite, "So, I hear you were up late last night?"

Their questions would be more concrete.

Because Joel McCreedy wasn't just a prodigal son, he was really a prodigal thief.

Chapter Two

"You've got some nerve."

The softly spoken words came from a source Joel knew well and one who stood blocking the school exit. Patsy Armstrong. She hadn't changed much in the last eight years. She looked like her two older daughters, tall, brunette, with a sturdy bearing that aged well.

Beth didn't look, or act, much like her mother.

Maybe that's why he hadn't recognized Beth right away last night? That, plus the fact she'd been four years behind him. He'd been in her oldest sister's graduating class.

"Hello, Mrs. Armstrong. I wondered if you were still working here."

Actually, he hadn't wondered. Until just this minute, she'd existed in the "out of sight, out of mind" realm of life. Joel was much too busy worrying about how Jared would react to forced hospitality. Jared's initial response—yesterday evening—had been the same as Mrs. Armstrong's.

You've got some nerve.

"I most certainly do still work here." Mrs. Armstrong wasn't finished. "I believe in an honest day's work for an honest day's pay."

Implying Joel didn't. She definitely wasn't one who would consider bull riding a profession, and it wouldn't matter how many purses Joel won or who his sponsor was. Bull riding didn't come with benefits like unemployment, a 401(k) or retirement. Not really.

The final bell rang. Joel could hear classroom doors opening and the excited clamor of student freedom, but Mrs. Armstrong wasn't finished. She just got louder. "Did you stop by the office and get a guest pass?"

"My nephews attend here."

"Your name is not listed on their student cards. You'll still need to sign in at the office. There just might be a problem."

A problem? The McCreedys had been attending this school since Joel's grandfather. Joel had not only studied here, but even when he was in high school, he'd helped out at the elementary school during the Rodeo Club events. The problem was Mrs. Armstrong.

"You going to send me to detention?" Joel knew the words would only make things worse, but he couldn't control his tongue.

She opened her mouth and narrowed her eyes. Joel just knew he didn't want to find out what she was thinking, so he did the first thing he could think of.

"I was here to return Beth's cell phone. Wish I'd thought to take down her number before I gave it back." He winked and moved around her toward the front door. Before exiting, he looked back. Mrs. Armstrong had closed her mouth but now had turned an interesting purplish color. Behind her, he could see Beth, two lines of students in her control.

Best place to be, safest place to be, thought Joel, would be the parking lot and inside his stepfather's minivan. He pushed open the school door and almost ran Billy down.

Joel recognized many of the adults, parents now, starting to gather in front of the school. His name floated on the air and a few scattered greetings sounded.

Nothing like what he had expected. What was wrong with Roanoke? Eight years wasn't that long.

"I thought I'd pick you up at the hospital," Billy said. Careful not to jar the small boy whose hand he was holding, Billy took Joel by the arm and drew him close so his words couldn't be heard by others. "Mind telling me what brought you to the school?"

"The hospital released me at noon and I took the truck to Tiny's garage. I had some papers to gather up and found Beth Armstrong's cell phone on the floorboard of my truck. Boy, she's really grown up to be—" Joel began.

"Mr. Staples," Patsy said, "I'm glad you're here. I need a minute."

Joel clearly and somewhat comically interpreted the look Billy shot him as, *Look, you've gotten me in trouble, too.*

Billy switched Caleb's hand to Joel's and then tossed him a set of keys. "Keep an eye on Caleb. Ryan and Matt will be out in a moment. Get them in the car and have them wait. I'll just be a minute."

Before Joel could protest, the chubby three-year-old tugged his fingers, looked up and said, "Let's go, Unca."

Unca?

At least Caleb was able to go with the flow. At Billy's nod, Beth released Matt, who walked toward Joel as if the weight of the world rested on his shoulders. Ryan, old enough to make his own exit, left his teacher and joined them. He didn't look too pleased about Joel's presence, either.

Not even twenty-four hours in town and Joel had managed to annoy everyone except Caleb. Joel figured he'd just broken a record, but knew there'd be no applause.

Ryan led the way to a minivan parked toward the back of the parking lot. To get to the car, Joel had to walk by people he'd once called friends. Most looked surprised. Some taken aback. Once his nephews—all little replicas of Jared—had stowed backpacks and secured their seat belts, Joel took his place on the passenger side.

With his truck needing repairs, Joel couldn't leave. With Joel himself needing repairs, Jared couldn't turn him away. Add to that the fact he had just enough money to get to the next town, some twenty miles away—well, no matter how you looked at it, storm clouds were gathering.

"So," came the beginning of a conversation from the backseat, "why did you take the money?" Oh, yes, Ryan was definitely his older brother's clone. Arms crossed, wasting no time, eyes accusing, Ryan wanted answers.

"What?"

"Some of my friends say you're a thief, that you stole money before you left town. Is that why you never came back? Is that why we don't know you? Why are you back now?"

Joel's experience with kids was almost nonexistent. He was pretty sure, though, that Ryan was a bit more mature—and cynical—than most eight-year-olds. Even so, Joel doubted that Ryan would understand that half of Solitaire Farm had, at one time, belonged to Joel, and that as a young, stupid kid, he'd wanted his share right then, in cash.

"I didn't steal any money. I took what was mine."

Ryan made a *psst* sound as Billy opened the driver's side door and slid behind the wheel. Wow. Joel was curious to know what Beth's mother had wanted to say, and why—as the school secretary—she had a right to say anything. Instead, he looked at the little men in the backseat and shelved his questions. Billy, looking a little annoyed, took advantage of the lull.

"What did the doctor say?"

"The doctor said the accident did not make things worse and that I feel better than I deserve after hitting that fence last night. He recommended a good physical therapist."

"You hit that fence really good." Ryan suddenly forgot his annoyance and sounded impressed. "Trey says it will cost a pretty penny."

"Trey?"

"Max McClanahan III," Billy explained.

The McCreedys' nearest neighbors were the McClanahans. Joel had spent his childhood chasing after Maxwell McClanahan II, who must be married and a dad now, with a son also named Max. One who was about Ryan's age. Joel suddenly felt a little humbled by all he didn't know.

"Joel never does anything halfway," Billy said before turning to face Joel. "I'm looking forward," he said glumly, "to hearing what's really wrong with you and what made you come back now."

"You have to go to a therapist because you hit a fence?" Ryan questioned. "I hit fences all the time. You do walk funny. Is that because you hit the fence?"

"Joel doesn't walk funny," Billy said.

"Just slow and careful," Joel agreed.

"Mommy couldn't walk at all," Matt finally added to the conversation, "right before she died."

"Okay," Billy said quickly, "who wants ice cream?"

To Joel's way of thinking, it was the perfect time to change the topic of conversation. Matt's comment was a bit too deep for an errant uncle to elaborate on. Looked like it was way too deep for a grandfather to deal with, too.

"Dad's not with us," Matt pointed out.

Ryan wasn't about to let that interfere with the possibility of getting ice cream. "We can take him something."

"It will melt."

Billy, who'd mastered the art of keeping kids happy during his forty-year stint as the principal, said, "He'll be eating plenty of ice cream tomorrow during Caleb's party."

"I'm three," Caleb chattered. "'Morrow."

Matt sat back, satisfied that his father wasn't being left out.

Joel had to admire him. He was the gatekeeper of the brothers. Ryan, it looked like, was the mouth. Caleb was the comic relief.

Jared didn't know how lucky he was.

Watching the boys sit forward on their hands, anticipating an ice cream stop, triggered some memories. Of course, back then, Jared had been the gatekeeper. Joel had been the comic relief. The one who had jumped over the gate, landed on his head and got all the attention.

They shared *mouth* duty.

Or tried to share.

Sometimes it had felt like the farm—make that the town of Roanoke—wasn't big enough for two Mc-Creedy boys.

Since his release from the hospital Joel had caught glimpses of his hometown and the people who made it special. In many ways, it was just another small town with its inhabitants going about their day, doing their jobs, taking care of their families and making memories. Since leaving eight years ago, Joel had been in towns a bit smaller and cities a lot bigger. He'd never stayed long enough to know who owned the auto repair shop, or even who was the fastest grocery store cashier, or which little old lady at church gave the best hugs, or what flavor ice cream was ordered the most at the ice cream parlor.

All three boys wanted chocolate. Billy chose vanilla.

Joel joined the boys and had chocolate, minus the cone. They ate inside the Ice Cream Shack because, according to Matt, "We can't drip in the car. Grandpa likes to keep his van clean."

"Caleb drips," Ryan agreed.

"I yike ice cream." Caleb nodded vigorously and lived up to Ryan's accusation. In just a matter of seconds, his ice cream cone was gone, but there was enough ice cream smeared on his face and on the floor to make another one. Ryan had just a bit on the side of his cheek. Joel took his last spoonful and looked over at Billy and Matt. Billy was making headway, but Matt was so careful not to drip or make any kind of mess that he almost had a full cone.

Then Matt stopped licking altogether. His eyes were glued on the front window and toward the parking lot.

Ryan gloated. "It's your teacher, and you have ice cream on your nose."

He didn't, but Matt believed him and rubbed his sleeve across his clean face.

Joel jumped up and held open the door. It gave him an even better view of his rescuer and Matt's teacher. Her blond hair bordered on white. It fluffed out and just hit the top of her shoulders. A dark blue skirt was topped by a white-and-dark-blue-striped blouse. Colorful tennis shoes finished the outfit.

He'd like to chase those tennis shoes. "Anything else change?" he asked.

She raised one eyebrow. "What?"

"Besides you growing up while I was away."

She hesitated. "I'm not as easy to get along with now."

"I don't believe it for a minute," Joel said, and checked out her hand, her left hand. No ring. He should have checked earlier.

"Let me buy you an ice cream." It wasn't exactly the dinner he'd suggested earlier, but she'd already turned that down. This could be a start.

Was it his imagination, or did the look she shot Billy appear sympathetic?

"Hi, Beth," Billy greeted, frowning in Joel's direction. "Looks like our paths are crossing quite a bit these last twenty-four hours."

"Susan called. She's wanting ice cream." Beth looked at Joel, her expression wary. "I'm in a hurry, so no thanks." Her chin went up, for no reason since he'd done nothing to insult her, and she headed to the counter. She ordered a full gallon of bubblegum.

Bubblegum? This might be her only flaw.

She followed that by ordering a chocolate chip cone. Joel stepped forward to pay, but she shook her head. The young man behind the cash register looked bored. Definitely not the kind of kid who would notice a guy trying to impress a girl and help him out.

"Bubblegum?" Joel questioned.

"Susan's pregnant. It's all she wants to eat. She puts blueberries on top." With that, Beth stopped paying attention to Joel, smiled at all three of the boys, especially Matt, and took a seat at the opposite end of the ice cream parlor. She pulled a book from her purse while she waited for her order.

"I feel like I struck out," Joel complained, "before I even made it to bat."

"What do you expect?" For the first time, Billy's usually calm demeanor slipped. He stared at Joel, an unwavering expression that said *talk, confess, convince.*

"I expected—" Joel carefully chose his words because his nephews, staring at him all big eyed and tense, didn't need to hear the family's dirty laundry

"—I expected to be able to say I was sorry and for all to be forgiven."

"That may take a bit of time."

"I was eighteen, an adult. Granted, I didn't leave in the most sensible manner. But I didn't expect for the whole town to treat me like a pariah."

To Joel's surprise, Billy didn't rush to assure him that everything was all right and his friends would come around. Instead, his stepfather's lips pursed together and a definite look of disappointment came over his expression.

"What?" Joel asked. "I chose the rodeo over the farm. It wasn't big enough for the two of us, anyway, and it was Jared's dream, not mine. Still, I should be able to come home for—"

"You boys stay put," Billy ordered. "Matt, finish your ice cream. Ryan, clean Caleb's face." He stood, motioning for Joel to follow him outside.

Joel stood too quickly, and then had to wait for his balance to return. All three boys looked at him like he was in trouble.

Beth still had her nose in her book.

The late-September sun still hovered high in the sky. A few cars were traveling down Main. Billy'd already made it to a distant picnic table. He sat with a rigid demeanor, his lips still pursed.

Joel waited, but Billy looked as if he expected Joel to do the talking.

The sunlight shimmered on the black-topped street in front of the Ice Cream Shack. Across from it was the barbershop where Joel had first climbed in a chair, sat on a padded seat with a cape over him and felt grown-up. Next door was the grocery store, not nearly as big as what the city boasted, but with a candy aisle that lived up to a preschooler's dreams. Everything looked the same; it was the feel of the place that had changed.

Fine. Joel would start. "Out with it, Billy," he ordered, carefully sitting across from his stepfather. "What's going on? I expected Jared to be mad, but to turn me away when I'm truly down on my luck? And people I waved to on the street this afternoon, they either waved back at me like I was a ghost or they didn't wave at all. At the school, I ran into people I grew up with, parents now, and they looked at me like I'm not real. Then Mrs. Armstrong practically tells me to never step foot in the elementary school again."

"You really don't know?" Billy asked.

"I. Really. Don't. Know."

"Maybe that knock on the head did permanent damage?" The words may have been in jest, but the look on Billy's face was serious.

"I really don't know what's going on," Joel repeated.

Billy looked at the sky, ran a hand over mostly nonexistent hair and sighed.

"It's one thing," Billy said, "to hurt people by taking what belongs to you."

Joel opened his mouth. He'd been stifled on the

farm, had always felt out of his element, and on top of everything else, Jared didn't want to share, especially after he'd married, brought his wife to Solitaire Farm to live and had a baby.

But Billy wasn't done. "It's quite another thing to hurt people by taking what *doesn't* belong to you."

The words hung in the air, an invisible yet tangible barrier between Joel and the stepfather he so admired. It hadn't been an easy decision, asking for his share of the inheritance, in dollars, instead of pitching in and staying on the family farm. But the will had stated that at eighteen Joel could sell his share. Because of the economy, it was a lot less than he'd expected. Still, Joel taking what was his hadn't caused the sale of Solitaire Farm; it had only caused a bigger mortgage.

"What? Are you saying the money you gave me didn't belong to me, because as I see it, having Jared buy me out was the best solution to—"

"I'm not talking about your half of the farm," Billy sputtered. "I'm talking about the Rodeo Club Fund."

Joel leaned forward, perplexed. "What about the RC money?"

Billy's expression took on a hard edge. "The money that I put in my office after the festival the night you left."

Joel growled, "I don't know what you're talking about. What about the RC money? I remember attending the Fall Festival because it was my last night in town, but—"

"I put it in my office," Billy said. "The treasurer said he figured we'd made double the usual. I was about to unlock the safe when my cell phone rang. One of the kids had gotten kicked by a horse. I didn't think twice. I took off."

That was Billy. He was a hands-on principal, and kids were his top priority.

"I took off," Billy continued. "About an hour later, I went back to the office. I'd never forgotten that I needed to lock that money away."

A bad feeling started prickling in Joel's stomach. This wasn't some proverbial story that Billy was telling to make a point.

"The money was gone," Billy said, "and so were you."

Joel had been sucker punched more than once in his twenty-six years, but never before had he realized that words had more impact than fists.

"You knew where I kept the key to my office, you knew I'd put the money in there, and you took it."

"I—" Joel opened his mouth in indignation, but finishing the conversation was not to be. They were no longer alone. Beth stood behind the three boys, her hand on Matt's shoulder.

"Matt's got a stomachache," she explained, her gaze going from Joel to Billy and back to Joel. To prove it, Matt held his stomach and doubled over a bit, moaning.

Beth shifted uncomfortably. "Is everything all right? Do you want me to run the boys home?"

"Everything's fine. Or, at least, it's going to be," Billy rushed to assure. His eyes never left Joel's face. Disappointment battled with anger.

Nothing was all right, not in Joel's life and apparently not in Matt's life, either.

Billy looked at Joel for a long moment before saying to the boys, "Let's head home before your father sends out the hunting dogs."

"We don't have any hunting dogs," Caleb complained.

"Shut up," Ryan said. He quickly and somewhat apprehensively looked at Billy, but instead of Billy offering the reprimand, it was Beth who chided, "Don't say *shut up,* say *be quiet.*"

"I might throw up," Matt added to the conversation. Because of the threat, apparently real, Matt rode shotgun in the front while Joel went in the back with Ryan and Caleb. Beth, with a backward glance, headed for her own vehicle. She clutched her ice cream in her arms.

Why he cared about her opinion so much, Joel didn't quite know. He needed to tell her, as well as Billy and apparently the whole town, that he was innocent.

No wonder lukewarm didn't begin to describe the way the town of Roanoke had responded to his return so far. Fundraising for the Rodeo Club Fund was tradition in Roanoke, going back fifty years. The Fall Festival was the Friday before Thanksgiving and put preschoolers on the back of sheep, brought a real carnival with a Ferris wheel and a roller coaster to town, and allowed the high school's marching band—usually about ten of them—to show off. It was fried chicken on picnic tables and a speech from the mayor.

Next to the Fourth of July celebration, it was the town's favorite, and the earnings helped with the cost of Roanoke's annual summer rodeo, where Joel's first taste of bull riding, at age eleven, led to big dreams and, later, exhilarating reality.

The whole town, as well as his family, thought him a thief. This probably, no, definitely, included Beth—although she hid it better—and her mother.

"Billy," Joel started. "Something's very wrong here. I didn't steal—"

"Little pitchers have big ears," Billy said. The three boys moved, but to prove Billy's point, Matt covered his ears. Ryan adopted an all-too-familiar judgmental look. One pretty advanced for a boy of eight.

The only forgiving one was Caleb. He clutched a raggedy napkin in one hand, held up two fingers with his other hand and informed Joel, "'Morrow. I be three."

"How about your truck?" Billy asked, settling behind the steering wheel and starting the van, effectively changing the subject again. His lips were still in a straight line. The smile that usually reached to his eyes was missing. It seemed for his grandchildren he was willing to put on an act and pretend nothing was wrong. Still Joel could only wonder...

maybe the question really was, *How soon will your truck be fixed so you can go?*

"I arranged to have it towed to Tiny's Auto Repair right after they checked me out of the hospital. He wasn't there. If possible, I'll stop by tomorrow morning. I think the door will be an easy fix, but I'm a little worried about the front bumper." Joel didn't really want to talk about his truck. More than anything, Joel wanted to protest his innocence.

He'd not stolen money from the elementary school's office, Billy's office, right before he left town. Thanks to his inheritance, half of the farm, Joel'd had a bank account in the six digits. At the time, he thought it would last forever.

"Tomorrow is Caleb's birthday," Matt reminded.

"I won't miss it."

If he was invited, that is. He'd not been invited to the house, not really, not by his brother. Billy was acting as the go-between and in just an hour, Joel would be facing a brother who did not want him home. Since Jared's weapon of choice had always been silence, a literal invitation seemed doubtful.

Chapter Three

❧

Beth's sister didn't even mention how melted the bubblegum ice cream was, just quickly got herself a bowl, grabbed the blueberries and motioned Beth to sit at the kitchen table.

Susan Farraday was a middle child suffering from oldest child syndrome.

"Linda called this morning."

Beth almost laughed, especially when Susan prepared a second bowl of blueberry-covered bubblegum ice cream and placed it in front of her.

"I'm full," Beth said.

Susan didn't say anything, just pulled the bowl back to her side of the table. "Tell me everything."

"About what?"

Susan's eyes narrowed. "Do you mean about *whom?*"

"There's nothing to tell. I went over to Solitaire Farm last night to talk to Jared about Matt. That didn't work. Mom wanted me to drop off some Bible study stuff to Meg McClanahan. I spent some time there eating watermelon and answering a few questions about Trey's homework even though he's not in my class."

Susan looked thoughtful. "Go on."

"On the way home, I noticed this truck ahead of me. It would speed up and then slow down. I was getting scared at first. Then I started trying to place it. I knew I'd seen it before. Finally, it really sped up, ran off the road, across the irrigation ditch and right into the McClanahans' fence."

"When did you realize it was Joel?"

"I think the moment I saw it, but I just didn't believe. Then, when I looked into the truck bed, his gear was back there."

"How is he?"

"He seems to be fine. He even helped pick up the boys from school."

"Does he look the same? Or cuter? Did he say anything about what he's been doing? I wonder if that means Jared's letting him stay?"

Beth thought back to the Ice Cream Shack and how tense a conversation she'd interrupted. They'd been talking about the RC money. "He was out of it while I drove him to the hospital. The only thing he said was that his head hurt. And I'm pretty sure he's staying, but last night he was sure leaving in a hurry. So, I doubt this visit is getting off to the best of beginnings."

"Is that all it is, a visit? Do you suppose he ran off the road because he and Jared had a fight?"

Beth had already considered that scenario, and it seemed plausible enough.

"Guess you'll know more tomorrow," Susan said. "Aren't you going to Caleb's birthday party?"

Beth had been there for all of Ryan, Matt and Caleb's special moments. As Mandy's best friend, she was a quasi aunt. A few minutes later, she headed for her car, grateful that Susan had failed to notice that Beth hadn't answered one of her previous questions.

Does he look the same? Or cuter?

Beth could never admit to her sisters that she thought Joel McCreedy looked even better than he had eight years ago. They'd known about her crush and had teased her without mercy. Susan might be seven months pregnant, Linda might own her own beauty salon, but that didn't stop them from ganging up on their baby sister, especially when it came to matters of the heart.

Especially when the matter of the heart had an arrow aimed at it, but not from Cupid's bow. Patsy Armstrong, aka Mom, was the sharpshooter in question.

The McCreedy men, all six of them if you counted stepfather Billy Staples, were having hot dogs for dinner. The kitchen hadn't changed all that much, except that Joel didn't know where he belonged. The table, from his childhood, was a six-seater, and Joel was pretty sure that the only vacant chair had at one time belonged to Mandy.

His sister-in-law had suffered with a long illness, was six months gone, and Joel hadn't made it to the funeral. He hesitated, and Billy came to the rescue. He got up, moved around the table and took the empty seat. Joel took Billy's place feeling like he kept winding up with the losing hand in a game with rules he didn't understand. Jared's and Matt's faces bore identical scowls when Joel sat down.

"So, what happened in school today?" Billy asked, unable to hide a look of resignation.

Matt didn't answer; he seemed to be contemplating.

"Were dere birfdays?" Caleb wanted to know.

Matt shook his head, but Ryan said, "There were no birthdays, but Trey took the bracelet that Mary got for her birthday and Mary had to chase him all around the playground."

Joel thought he saw a slight smile hit Jared's face, even though Jared didn't seem willing to add to the conversation.

"How about you?" Billy encouraged. "Did you see Trey chasing Mary?"

"No," Matt admitted, "but I saw him get in trouble. Miss Armstrong made him sit out the rest of recess."

Ryan and Caleb finished their food within minutes. Ryan took out a homework paper. Caleb went into the living room to admire the two giant bags of birthday decorations that he promised not to touch.

After a moment, Ryan shouted, "Done!" and headed for the living room to tease his little brother about the birthday present bandit.

Billy looked at Matt, who'd taken two tiny bites of his hot dog and totally ignored the fries. "You don't need to clean your plate tonight."

Joel couldn't tell who was more surprised: Matt or Jared.

Maybe Matt. He looked at his grandpa without moving.

"Go ahead," Jared urged, adding to the conversation for the first time.

Still, Matt dragged his feet. Finally, Jared held up a finger. "One." Then up went another finger. "Two." Matt's plate made it to the sink on four; he made it out the kitchen door on five.

Without the boys, the room took on an uncomfortable quiet.

Billy didn't waste a minute. In a serious tone, he began, "Joel and I were talking after I picked up the boys. We didn't get a chance to finish."

Jared didn't even question about what, just gave Joel a suspicious and unwelcoming look.

"First," Billy said, "why don't you tell us what brought you home."

The expression on Billy's face didn't change. He'd been a principal for more than forty years and told anybody willing to listen that "he'd seen it all." He'd been a successful principal because while he'd seen it all, he was still willing to listen.

Jared didn't say anything. His lips were puckered in a straight line that Joel recognized. He didn't really care what Joel had to say, just wanted Joel out of here and for things to go back to normal. Listening to his little brother was so low on his list of priorities that it wasn't a priority at all.

"I should have stayed in New Mexico." Joel didn't mean it, though. Something about being in his childhood kitchen, seeing the school papers held by magnets on the fridge, and sitting at the table where he'd helped his mom make cookies and in turn his mom had helped him with homework, something about it all made him catch his breath and consider what he'd given up.

"You keep up with my career?" Joel asked.

Jared shook his head, but Billy said, "You've been a midlister for quite a while."

A midlister, not a rodeo term but definitely a retired teacher term, felt like a grade of C. "I'm only eight years in," Joel said. "I still have at least ten years of competition ahead of me."

Jared gave a half snort.

"The highest standing you've managed to reach is fifty," Billy said.

"And that kind of standing has earned me enough money to stay in the show even after the seed money was spent."

Jared tensed. The seed money might have been Joel's half of the farm, but in Jared's mind, the farm needed it more than Joel.

Billy held up his hand, halting the dialogue. "This is not the conversation I meant to have. What exactly brought you home? I read that you were injured, but I don't recall which rodeo or what happened."

"I was in Lovington, New Mexico, just over a month ago. I did fine, came in third and took home a purse of just under two thousand dollars. I was supposed to meet up with some friends in Missouri after that, but the morning I was to leave, the Monday after the rodeo, I had a hard time getting out of bed. I was as stiff as I'd ever been."

"You came in third, so you kept your seat," Billy remembered.

"That I did. The only thing I can figure is I must have landed wrong, hurt myself and not even realized it."

"What do you mean?"

"I mean that I went to bed fine, woke up stiff that morning and by evening, a buddy literally carried me to the truck and drove me to the emergency room. I've never hurt so much. I couldn't move to the left or right without nauseating pain. Doctor there said acute lumbar strain and vertebrae damage. For a solid week, I was in bed, in a lonely motel room. After that, I started physical therapy, and everything seemed to be going great. I could bend, jump and even lift. Then, after about two weeks of that, I was walking toward the motel room and I can't even describe what it felt like, except that my back did a little break-dance of its own without my permission. Just like that, I was back in bed and on pain pills. After a week, I realized I couldn't do it on my own."

"And that's when you decided to come home," Billy figured.

Joel looked at Billy and then at his brother. On Billy's face was an expression of concern. Jared's face, however, remained suspicious.

"It seemed like a good idea at the time."

"You were right to come home," Billy said.

Looking at Jared, Joel continued, "This is truly the strangest injury I've ever had. One day I feel like I could possibly jump on the back of a bull and do the eight-second ride, the next day I'm wondering if I can make it to the bathroom."

"So basically," Jared stated, looking at Billy and not at Joel, "he's coming home because he needs help but he can't be of any help."

"I—" Joel started.

"—always have a home here," Billy said firmly. "I won't lie. I'm having a hard time forgiving how you literally ran away, how few times you called and how you never came home when we needed you."

"I didn't find out about Mandy until it was too late," Joel started. "I would—"

"No excuses. We're done." Billy looked at Jared. "The Bible's very clear. It's about time you dust yours off. Joel is family, and Jesus clearly states in the fifth chapter of First Timothy that *'if anyone does not provide for his relatives, and especially for his immedi-*

ate family, he has denied the faith and is worse than an unbeliever.'"

Jared did not look repentant. "The Bible also says, *'Thou shalt not steal.'"*

Joel felt his teeth clench. What was most amazing was that in eight years, the family had so tiptoed around this ridiculous accusation that it was the first time he'd heard of it. "I didn't steal."

"Joel was about to tell me his side of what happened to the RC money," Billy spoke up, "but then Matthew got sick to his stomach and Beth Armstrong interrupted us."

"I can't believe you think I would steal money."

"It's no secret that you thought your half of the farm was worth more," Jared said.

"True, but I also thought—okay, dreamed—that I'd be looking at career winnings of over a million dollars. You heard me say that for years. I got my Professional Rodeo Cowboys' Association card right before I left. I believed so strongly in my dream. Plus, you knew I felt guilty taking what I did. That's why I left the way I did."

"Every little bit helps," Jared quoted their father.

"I didn't take the RC money," Joel said again, not that Jared was listening. Billy, though, finally looked a little more thoughtful than stoic.

"Twelve thousand, three hundred and seventy-four dollars," Jared stated.

"You have the amount memorized?" Joel asked, incredulous, looking at his big brother.

"Of course I do." Jared stood. Carefully, methodically, he put his dinner plate and glass in the kitchen sink. Then, as he walked out the door, he added, "I reimbursed the club so they wouldn't press charges."

Outside, the whir of a combine penetrated the murkiness that made up Joel's slumber. He kept his eyes tightly closed, hoping the headache would disappear and sleep would return. It didn't.

The bed was harder than it needed to be, but maybe that was just an effect of the pain in every bone in Joel's body. Especially his head. Great, until the night before last the only thing that hadn't hurt was his head. Opening one eye, Joel winced and took in his surroundings and noted the time. Wide awake at seven on a Saturday morning. Who needed an alarm clock? Pain worked better and didn't offer a snooze option.

He slowly opened the other eye.

The guest room hadn't really changed in the last fifteen years, not since his mother had decorated it in a fit of Martha Stewart enthusiasm and a good crop year. Both his parents were gone now—his dad while Joel was still in elementary school to a tractor mishap, his mom to cancer the year he turned eighteen. When she died, Joel lost his footing. The only thing he'd wanted was to leave because he no longer felt like he belonged.

But maybe he'd left because it hurt to belong.

Their memory dimmed as Joel eased up to a sitting

position. He managed to get one leg to the ground, and while he rested he stared at the only thing new in the room, a sewing machine. It must have belonged to Jared's late wife, Mandy. Come to think of it, right before Jared's wedding, there'd been a bunch of Mandy's friends gathered in the living room doing something to the curtains with those plastic things that came with cola six-packs. Two years later, right before Joel left, Mandy and her best friends had been sitting in the same living room, the one that now had prettier curtains, making baby blankets.

Had Beth been there? He tried to remember and finally, after thinking of all the times he'd hung around with Beth's sisters, a memory surfaced. She'd been there, but not to sew. She offered advice a time or two, but just as often as not, when Joel came through the room, she'd been reading. He remembered now.

No wonder he hadn't realized what a beauty she was. She'd been so young and always had her head down with her nose stuck in a book.

He put both hands, palms down, on the bed and pushed. He stood, winded and then sat down again as the knob on the bedroom door started to turn. He'd left the hospital yesterday feeling good on whatever they'd pumped him full of. Today wasn't going to be such a feel-good day.

He heard a few snickers and maybe some pushing, and finally the door inched open. More snickering and then, as though he'd been pushed, Caleb hurtled in and stumbled to a halt. Two fingers were in his mouth, shoved deep enough to hurt.

"Morning, Caleb," Joel greeted. "Are you being shy today?"

The fingers didn't come out of his mouth and Caleb didn't respond.

From the doorway came a whispered command, "Tell him it's time for breakfast. Tell him Grandpa said."

But, as youngest sons are prone to do, this one didn't listen, just shook his head again.

"It's time for breakfast." The door opened all the way and Ryan came in. He gave his little brother a dirty look. "Grandpa said. And Caleb's not shy, he's just being stubborn."

The words may have come from an eight-year-old's mouth, but they were Jared's words, complete with tone. The way Joel had heard them, all those years ago, was more like, "I'm Jared, the oldest. And Joel's off hiding somewhere because he doesn't want to do the real work. He's just being lazy." Real work was driving the tractor, not making sure it worked. Real work was spending eight hours straight harvesting, not spending eight seconds on a bull for a chance at a couple thousand dollars and a buckle.

Jared and Joel had different ideas of fun.

Matt peeked through the door, not willing to enter, but not willing to miss out on what was happening. "Matt *is* shy," said Ryan. Matt neither disagreed nor entered the room.

"I'm three." Caleb took the two fingers from his mouth and held them up.

"He's three," Ryan agreed. "And after we eat, Grandpa wants you to help set up his party."

Joel managed to stand once again.

"You not staying?" Caleb asked, moving closer.

"Dad says you're leaving soon," Ryan agreed. "And we're not supposed to talk to you except when we have to."

"Grandpa says he's staying," Matt reminded from the doorway. "Until he's better."

"I'm not sure what I'm doing," Joel said.

"He's staying." Grandpa Billy put his right hand firmly on Matt's shoulder. "And you boys are leaving. It's past time for you two to be doing your chores."

Billy hadn't made a sound as he walked down the hallway. Years of being an elementary school principal had taught him how to sneak up on kids. Ryan and Caleb giggled. Matt pretty much harrumphed, sounding more like Grandpa Billy than a mere boy. After a moment, they all left.

Joel put a hand to his head. He wasn't sure if it was his nephews' visit or the passing of time, but his headache was gone. Outside he could hear the tractor shutting down and the boys shouting, "Morning, Dad." At least some things didn't change.

He felt a pull in his lower back, but it was only a dull ache, not a blinding pain that flashed every time he so much as twitched. You'd think the minor traffic accident would have made things worse. Instead, it was just another day of not knowing if he'd be bed-ridden or moving.

That's what happened with acute lumbar strain and multiple vertebra damage.

He heard the tractor start again and quickly die. He heard another vehicle, too, and at first thought it was Billy driving away. Instead, an engine turned off and someone, maybe Ryan, shouted, "Hey."

Joel went to the window and opened the curtains wide. Max McClanahan II was already heading toward Jared. Joel could just imagine the gist of their conversation.

Max would be saying something like, "How fast were you chasing Joel when he hit our fence?"

And Jared might be saying, "If I'd been chasing him, he'd be gone. How much damage and what's the cost?"

Nope, Joel didn't need any help imagining the conversation happening right under his window, especially when he saw Max extend his arms wide and laugh.

Guess there wasn't just a small hole in that fence. Jared didn't laugh in return. Just shook his head. Joel couldn't believe he'd neglected to get Billy to show him the damage yesterday. Five bucks. That's all Joel had. And, in just a little over the past twenty-four hours, he'd managed to add more hospital bills and now a fence.

"Dad, I gotta go potty!" A small boy opened the door to Max's truck. A little girl tried to scamper behind, but was caught in the seat belt until Billy went over to help her out of it. Max raised a hand, signaling for the little boy to head for the house.

No, very little had changed at Solitaire Farm. True to form, Joel was the last one out of bed. And, by the time he made it downstairs, Max and his kids had already headed back home.

Twenty years ago, Max had considered the Mc-Creedy home as his and popped over on a whim. Jared and Joel had done the same at the McClanahan place. Max's mother was the best cook in Iowa. All through school, Max had been one grade above Joel and one grade behind Jared. He'd been the class clown, always struggling to make it through with Cs, never making first string and he was the first of their group to notice hair loss.

Judging by the smile on his face when he looked at the two kids, none of that mattered anymore. His life was going pretty well. No doubt, in Roanoke, Iowa, quite a lot about his high school friends had changed in the last eight years. They were planting families, growing careers and harvesting community.

They were also all older and wiser, while Joel had just gotten older.

Chapter Four

Saturday afternoon, Beth parked behind a parade of cars and followed her sister Linda across the driveway and up to Solitaire Farm's porch. Susan had wanted to crash the party along with Linda, but the smell of birthday cake made her ill. However, bubblegum ice cream topped with blueberries made her happy. Go figure. Susan enjoyed being pregnant entirely too much.

A banner tied between two ceiling slates promised a Rootin' Tootin' Birthday. The door was propped open with a train, and inside the living room was scattered a handful of parents, more than Beth expected to see. The only parent missing was Jared.

With the way Matt had been acting yesterday, half in awe and half afraid of Joel, Beth didn't want to wait any longer before speaking to Jared. She hated using a kid's birthday party for a parent-teacher conference, but Jared had a knack for avoiding issues.

Mona Gabor smiled and waved Beth over, but Beth pointed to the back door. "Is Jared outside?"

Mona shook her head. "He's down at Solitaire's Market, no doubt hoping a few of the parents will stop and make a purchase or two."

Solitaire's Market had been Mandy's idea. They'd started the roadside store about the time Matt was born. To everyone's surprise, it made money. Beth knew because she'd worked in it many a Saturday, helping out.

The market was just one more thing on Jared's plate. When Mandy was alive, Jared had cared about making sure his family was provided for, but not so that he'd missed being a part of their everyday lives. Now that Mandy was gone, Jared obsessed about work to such an extent that Billy had become his sons' primary caregiver. Beth edged toward the kitchen and a clean getaway. Mona tended to ask a lot of questions.

Before Beth could make it to the backyard, she heard Billy say, "Is there a hole in it?"

"I don't know yet." Joel, standing in the middle of what looked like a deflated hot-air balloon, nodded at Beth as she came out the back door. Then, as if suddenly realizing who she was, sent her a full-blown smile. He was wearing loose jeans and a tight blue T-shirt that had seen better days. He actually looked like he was having fun amid all the chaos.

He was looking at her as if she just added to the fun.

"It came with a repair kit," Billy said, totally missing out on his helper's inattention.

Joel looked at home in the backyard. That shouldn't surprise her; after all, he'd grown up on Solitaire Farm. He stood all handsome and strong looking. She wouldn't have recuperated so quickly if she'd driven her car into a fence and suffered a concussion.

He made no move to patch the inflatable jump house. Instead, he asked, "Did you bring a book to read?"

She was surprised he remembered. "No, I didn't bring a book to read."

He shook his head. "You even read during football games."

"Quit jabbering," Billy ordered, as a little girl ran and hid behind him to avoid being caught by Mona Gabor's three-year-old. "Fix the hole so we can get these kids occupied." A moment later, the Gabor toddler plowed into Billy, almost knocking him to the ground and inspiring Joel to get busy.

Beth watched him, noting the way his hair rippled in the wind, how his body moved—just a bit on the hesitant side—and how easily he fixed the leak.

That was his gift, always, even more than sports. He tinkered, on the farm, at school and at Tiny's garage. All those years ago, when she'd been watching him from afar and thinking he didn't notice her, maybe he had.

A tiny piece of her—one she didn't dare let grow *because of all the what ifs*—felt exhilarated.

In their small Iowa town, high school football rated

as one of the top three things to do—right after *go to church* and *take care of the family*. She'd started going to games when she was eleven. About the time she hit thirteen, she'd had enough. She wasn't going to follow her sisters' Adidas athletic shoes onto the field and wave pom-poms. Being in the limelight never appealed to Beth. Until Joel had made quarterback, she'd sat on the bleachers—there to support both her sisters, who were cheerleaders—with her nose in a book while those around her cheered. Of course, the stadium lights didn't make for easy reading, and it had seemed like every time Beth got comfortable, the bleachers moved. Everyone wanted to stomp their feet in tune with the cheerleaders. If they weren't doing that, they'd stand to either cheer a good call or debate a bad one.

When Joel had made quarterback, she'd read her book but she'd made sure to watch when he played. She'd always considered him worth watching. Only once before had she noticed him watching back. It was the game-winning play, his senior year. She'd seen his teammates lifting him in the air. He'd whipped off his helmet and looked into the crowd.

Right at Beth.

Or so it had seemed.

Then he'd been swallowed up not only by his teammates, but by the cheerleaders, coaches and fans.

And Beth had returned to her book.

Looking at Joel McCreedy now, with the sunlight dancing in his hair and laughter dancing in his eyes, she almost felt weak-kneed. Obviously, schoolgirl crushes didn't go away, even when the object of the crush moved far, far away.

No doubt about it, books were a safer investment than Joel McCreedy. The last time he'd left, he'd not known he was taking her heart. All it would take was one touch, the right word and that full-blown come-hither grin, and everyone would know he could win her heart.

Including her mother.

And since Joel had no staying power, she'd be here in Roanoke picking up the pieces all by herself again.

No, thank you.

Joel straightened, watching as Beth made her way to a group of adults busy setting out the makings for a hot dog and potato chip meal. Her red-and-white-striped shirt topped tight jeans that fell midknee. White socks and white tennis shoes finished off the look.

Definitely a target to follow.

He was careful not to move too quickly. He'd already made a mistake or two today. First, he'd picked up Caleb so he could watch as people parked in the driveway. Apparently, to a three-year-old, watching friends arrive with presents was almost as good as getting to open the presents.

Picking Caleb up hadn't hurt, but putting him down had.

His next mistake was helping Billy put up the jump house. The whole experience had to do with bending over and straightening up—two things he should really only do in moderation or at the physical therapist's office.

Or so said the doctor Joel had visited after getting the diagnosis about the acute lumbar strain. The doctor, a sports medicine specialist, highly recommended, had said over and over, "An injury like this never goes away. One wrong move, awkward turn, and suddenly walking from the couch to the bathroom will take an hour. You'll always have pain, but if you're careful, you can lead a normal life."

Careful meant avoiding the bull; *normal* didn't include the rodeo.

"We have exercises that will help you get stronger," the physical therapist had agreed.

Riding a bull *was exercise* and Joel had always been strong.

"You can still ride," the doctor had emphasized, "but I strongly recommend horses, not bulls, and not in competition, but for pleasure.

"If you do your exercises, especially the stretches," the physical therapist encouraged.

Until just this moment, Joel had been focusing on the things he didn't want to do: Ride a horse instead of a bull. Exercise because he had to. Return, tail tucked under, to Solitaire Farm.

Finding out most of the town thought he was a thief was just one more nail in the coffin holding his dreams.

Right now, though, the only dream he needed to be thinking of was Caleb's. As if in response to that thought, Billy shouted, "I need help!"

Billy's words were more an order; Joel had been doing grunt work from the moment he'd finished breakfast. Getting ready for a three-year-old's birthday party was harder than preparing for an eight-second ride. And, surprise, surprise, Joel had enjoyed every minute—except for the occasional unwelcome stiffness from the ever-present back pain.

Joel also was enjoying watching Beth traipse across the lawn. Joel followed her movements all the way to a group of people and a guy Joel didn't know. She put her hand on his arm and starting talking. The guy nodded and soon what looked to be a serious conversation started. Joel took one step toward her, then another. He stopped when her sister Linda wandered outside and in just a matter of moments landed in the midst of a bunch of her girlfriends—laughing and trying to outtalk each other with animated arm gestures. Joel wondered where Susan, the other sister, was. They usually weren't far apart.

He looked back at Beth. She didn't need to laugh out loud. Ever the little lady, her eyes did the laughing for her. Joel took another step. She might be talking to a strange man, but she was aware of Joel.

He knew how to recognize hooded looks and practiced nonchalance.

Every few seconds a kid would come over and wrap his or her arms around Beth's leg.

The woman was now a kid magnet.

As he took another step, he figured that maybe she was a man magnet, too.

He almost felt propelled to join them. No doubt about it. Beth was definitely a Joel magnet.

Without a second thought, Joel joined the crowd of two.

The man eyed Joel warily, not in a tired manner, more with a guarded hesitation. He looked young, too young. Still, when he spoke, he didn't beat around the bush. "So, you're the infamous Joel McCreedy."

"That would be me."

"I hear you went eight seconds against a fence and the fence won."

"Can't help what you draw." Joel stuck out his hand. "And you are?"

Judging by the look in the other man's eyes, Joel recognized competition, a worthy opponent.

"Nathan Fisher. I'm the new youth minister at the Main Street Church. I've been in Roanoke about a year."

Maybe, just maybe, Joel surmised, Nathan might be one of a handful of people who didn't already judge Joel a thief.

Mona Gabor chose that moment to join them.

She held her three-year-old balanced on one hip and didn't seem to notice that said child had a messy hunk of birthday cake in his hands and was waving electric-blue-frosting-covered fingers dangerously close to her hair.

Beth gently took the piece, not even noticing when blue frosting dripped on her pants, and fed it to the kid.

"Thanks," Mona said without taking her eyes off Joel. "Did you get any buckles?"

Beth looked curious, too. Funny, all the time he'd been on the road, he'd imagined his family and friends back home keeping track.

Instead, they'd been going about the business of living their lives. "Yes, I won a few buckles."

Her eyes widened. "How many?"

"Fifteen. I've got fifteen buckles." What he didn't add was that you couldn't pay bills with buckles and how quickly his half of the farm money had disappeared. He didn't add that even with fifteen wins, he'd not pulled in any sponsors. Oh, he'd earned more than his fair share of decent-sized purses, too. They'd financed the next rodeo and the next and the next. He'd come close to being part of the crowd aiming to become national champions. Close, however, wasn't a word that meant much when your belly was empty and you were sharing a room with three other cowboys all comparing the war wounds of their chosen career.

Because serious bull riding was a career. One that

Joel had studied for, longed for, lived and ached to return to.

"Have you ever been on television?" Mona today was much the same as Mona eight years ago. She had plenty of questions. He could only hope she didn't bring up the missing money. Or, maybe he should hope she would, so he could proclaim his innocence.

Then he remembered Caleb shouting "I'm three. I'm three!" No, this was Caleb's day.

"Did you ever meet the guy they made that movie about?" Mona asked. "You know, the one..."

There were quite a few rodeo movies, but answering Mona's question would only spur more questions of the same ilk. He decided to head her off at the pass. "Besides the buckles," he continued, "I also met some incredible people, not movies stars, but real people. People who've made a difference, like..."

But she'd already stopped listening. She was just one more person who only cared about the buckles and the headlines, proof that the hometown boy made good. She didn't know or care about the amazing people he'd met. Before Joel could think of something else to say, she turned away and started talking to someone else.

Immediately, his eyes sought out Beth, but she'd disappeared while he'd been musing about the past.

Which left Joel alone with Nathan Fisher, who had the same half smile on his face that little Matt wore most of the time.

"So," Joel, who couldn't stand the silence, said, "how did you get lucky enough to be invited to Caleb's birthday party?"

"My sister baked the cake. She started a catering business. I volunteered to deliver."

Joel figured there was more, so he waited. Sure enough, Nathan continued. Leaning in, he said in a hushed tone, "I was also hoping to get the chance to speak with your brother. Make an effort to personally invite him to church."

"Jared's stopped going to church?" Joel had halfway expected Nathan to say something about Beth, something like "keep away," or, "You look pretty good for a man who wrestled a fence and lost," or at the least issue a few questions like "How long are you staying?"

Before Joel could ask questions, someone shouted Joel's name, and the opportunity was lost.

"Man, it's good to see you. You look tired." Trust his one-time best friend, Derek Livingston, to state the obvious. Clasping Derek's hand in a sturdy shake for the briefest of moments, Joel experienced what he'd expected to experience every time he saw an old friend.

Homecoming.

With Derek, there was a repeat of that welcome. Still, the most Joel could muster was, "I am tired. Good to see you."

"I'm sorry you're back *this way.* I expected you to ride into town in a parade."

"Yeah, well, my parade's over and I should have aimed my float home a long time ago. What about you?"

"I'm doing great." Derek laughed. "And speaking of floats, I help with the annual Roanoke Rodeo Club Parade now. My work sponsors it."

"Work?" Joel shook his head. "You're not working with your dad?"

"You do what you got to do, as you well know. I'm vice president of the Roanoke Bank." Together, the two men scanned the backyard, before Derek finally admitted, "I'd forgotten how it feels to be on the outskirts of town, with plenty of land and animals. Dad sold his place four years ago when he retired. He offered it to me, but I said no. Looking at my kids," Derek continued, "makes me regret that decision."

"Which kids are yours?" Joel asked, not that he needed to. Earlier inside the house, Joel had watched as two black-headed boys, stocky, had already followed Ryan up the stairs to his room and then down the stairs for food and then up the stairs for more playing and then down the stairs for more food.

"Twins?" Joel asked.

"Yep, I have the two boys, and my wife's home with our littlest." Derek's eyes lit up, much the way they had back when they'd been winning football games. "Our little girl's two weeks old today."

So far, everyone—well, everyone he'd run into

during the last forty-eight hours—from Joel's past, save Beth and her sister Linda, came with a kid or two in tow. Some were already taller than the fence post.

"Unca, I want up." Caleb crashed into Joel's legs and practically started climbing. Right behind him was a little girl. Caleb didn't really want up; he wanted to get away from the little girl.

"Not right now," Joel said. "Maybe later when everyone's gone and we go inside."

"He'll be asleep the moment the last partygoer heads out," Derek predicted, as his cell phone went off and he headed for a quiet area. Joel could hear the beginnings of, "Hey, babe, is everything all right?"

Derek, unlike Joel's brother, was willing to start up right where they'd left off: best friends.

Closer than brothers.

He didn't even mention the eight years that had passed without a phone call or visit. He didn't mention the missing money.

Joel headed inside to look for Beth. She was wiping frosting from her pants but before Joel could reach her, he spotted Matt standing against the wall. The five-year-old looked miserable and every few seconds he'd raise up on his toes and jiggle a bit.

The bathroom had a line, and Matt wasn't in it. Plus, for some reason, the more-than-a-century-old farmhouse still boasted only one full bathroom on the first floor.

That would have been the first change, had Joel

stayed on. He moved toward Matt but stopped when Cindy Turner stepped in front of him. Blond headed, tallest of all the girls he'd run with, she was also the loudest and, yes, the most fun.

"What I want to know," she said, "is how you managed to stay single? What's wrong with all those buckle bunnies?"

He glanced at her finger. She obviously wasn't single, so her last name probably was no longer Turner unless she'd added one of those fancy hyphens to her name.

"I guess I was busy," Joel quipped for lack of any other response.

"No." The word was spoken in a deep, serious voice. The room's noise faded as if someone had turned down the stereo.

Joel stood straighter, even though it hurt, and looked at his older brother.

"No," Jared repeated. "I'm the one who was busy." And then, after he dropped the bomb, he left the room.

"He was busy," Cindy whispered, "and after Mandy died, he made sure he was so busy that when people stopped by, they'd feel guilty for interrupting him. He's even stopped coming to church. If it weren't for the kids…"

When she saw that Joel wasn't going to add anything else, Cindy also slipped away.

The party skipped a beat, regrouped, and soon the kids were happily either playing in the jump house or chasing each other while the adults were eating and laughing again—sitting in pairs or cliques talking about their past, their present day and their futures. Joel only knew about their past. He was quickly figuring out their present. It was the future he was uncertain about, like always. In some ways it was like a giant hand had plucked him out of this world, deposited him in another and, when he had failed at that world, put him back where he'd started.

Only, in this world he had an asterisk next to his name that he hadn't earned.

Joel didn't get to delve too long on the issue of the stolen money because again he noticed Matt, still standing in the hallway, still jiggling, only now his face was a pure grimace. This time when Joel moved, no one stepped in his way. He made it to Matt's side, bent down, regretted the move and straightened some, then whispered in his nephew's ear, "Need to use the bathroom?"

For a moment, he thought Matt wasn't going to respond.

Then Joel offered his hand. Slowly Matt nodded. Together they walked to the backyard and out behind the barn to an old oak tree far from the party.

"Out here?" Skeptical didn't begin to describe the look on Matt's face. "Grandpa Billy says only if it's a 'mergency."

"We'll call this an emergency," Joel urged.

A moment later, Matt proved that it indeed had been an emergency. Then, without a word, Matt shoved his hands in his pants pockets and with an air of dejection headed back for the house.

Joel followed, making sure Matt stayed outside where the kids were playing instead of holing up in a watchful corner. The kid needed a life.

"Good job, Uncle." Beth was in the backyard, gathering up messy paper plates and half-full paper cups.

"Hey." He sauntered over and started grabbing errant napkins and plastic forks, all the while ignoring the stiffening in his back and looking at the woman who just might make coming home more than bearable.

She shook her head, her blond hair fanning out in gentle waves, as if she knew something he didn't. Right now, her eyes, a shade of forest green, darkened as she assessed him.

"Don't worry. Jared will come back to church. He just has to come to terms with Mandy's death."

"How did you know what I was thinking?"

"I overheard Nathan talking to you. I saw the look on your face."

"Jared always went to church. He'd even give up other opportunities to attend." What Joel didn't say, but what was already occurring to him, was how little he'd gone to church and how he'd not known how to grieve after his mother died.

He'd left rather than face the pain. He'd left instead of fighting. On the bull, he always knew the goal and could reach the goal. Here on Solitaire Farm, it had always seemed like the goal kept changing.

"Family means more to him than it does to you," Beth said. "Always has."

Joel opened his mouth to argue but didn't know what to say, and in the silence that followed, Beth shook her head and walked off, disappearing into the kitchen.

She was wrong. Family meant a great deal to Joel. He'd always wanted to make his parents proud. It was just, well, Jared always got there first. Even when Joel did the same things—got straight As, hit the home run that won the game, earned an award from Future Farmers of America—Jared had already been there, done that and worn the T-shirt.

Joel hated being second best.

The only thing Joel had been good at that Jared wasn't was bull riding.

And the only thing Jared was good at that Joel wasn't was farming.

Farming paid the bills. It was the lifeblood of the McCreedys. Bull riding cost money. Of course, it also provided the type of memories a man could take to the grave smiling.

But it could be an early grave.

Chapter Five

From the time Beth had hit the toddler stage, she'd loved barns, her favorite being the one at her grandparents' place. That barn, painted the required rustic red, had housed a cow so tame it followed her around like a pet dog.

Her grandparents were gone and so was their farm. It was now a dollar store. Still, progress and new buildings were proof that life went on. Something Jared needed to realize.

She found him in the barn, avoiding the party, and probably wishing like crazy that Mandy were here to organize the day and make sure he knew his role.

Without Mandy, he couldn't seem to get it right. Worse, to Beth's way of thinking, he wasn't even trying, and that wasn't going to last long, if she had her way.

"Get a lot of business down at the market?"

Jared didn't look at her. "Not really."

Beth waited a moment, hoping he'd say something

first. When he didn't, she started, "We've been in school for almost a month, and I'm not seeing any improvement in Matt's attitude," Beth said gently. "He doesn't want to be in school. He acts unhappy, and for the most part, he's unwilling to try. He scribbles his name. At recess, he sits on the bench by whichever teacher is on duty. At lunch, he won't eat unless forced. His success in school depends on you taking an active role."

Jared leaned against the wooden slats that kept his horse penned. He stared at the bay for a solid minute. Beth knew because she counted to sixty before he responded, "I don't know what to do. After you left, Thursday, I tried talking to him."

Beth knew a two-minute conversation, make that a scolding, to a five-year-old was one thing; a consistent, everyday example was another. She swallowed. This was the part of the job she didn't enjoy and one she didn't feel confident about.

Who was she to tell parents what to do? She didn't even have children. She hadn't walked a mile in their shoes, and she was only beginning her second year out of college. "Yesterday I sent home a letter about the Fall Festival. I asked for parent volunteers. Billy's helping, I know that. I'm hoping you'll take part?"

Jared's lack of response told Beth all she needed to know. So far this weekend, he, personally, hadn't opened his son's backpack to see what was in it. He hadn't read her newsletter telling him about the festival, or about what letter of the alphabet the class was working on, or about Show and Share.

Disengaged, that's what her teacher mentor would call Jared.

It was a fine line she walked. Right now, she was an elementary school teacher, nothing more. She wasn't a counselor. She didn't have to be one to see the kind of hurt Jared's family suffered. But, boy, she'd love to have more of an idea about how to help.

"I'll talk to him," Jared promised, pushing away from the pen and heading toward the barn's door without waiting to see if she followed. Behind her, his horse snorted. Beth almost wanted to do the same. She'd accomplished nothing, and judging by his quick steps, he didn't want her company.

She doubted he was heading to find the backpack. More likely he just wanted to be alone.

Jared had barely faded into the early-evening sun when a figure stepped into the barn's open door. For a moment, Beth thought Jared had changed his mind. Then the shadow moved, limping slightly, and stepped into the light. "What's happening with Matt?" Joel asked.

Tempted as she was to spill everything, schools nowadays preached privacy, and unless Jared gave her permission to share with Joel, Beth couldn't do it.

"Tell me." Joel moved closer until he stood next to her. Unlike Jared, he didn't lean against the stall. He stood straight, towering over Beth, and stared at her rather than the horse. His voice was seductive instead of angry.

She swallowed again. This time sorrow had nothing to do with it. It was pure feminine reaction. Unwelcome. "You'll need to ask Jared."

"Basically," Joel drawled, "that's not an option. My brother's way of expressing anger is to stop talking. So far, he's only said a few words to me and none of them involved brotherly bonding."

Beth could just imagine how well Jared was reacting to Joel's sudden appearance.

"Of course—" Joel's eyes glittered, acorn hard and rock smooth "—he said 'good' when he thought I might be leaving."

"The last few years haven't been easy," Beth said gently.

"Tell me something I don't know."

"I'd be wasting my time since you'll be gone before Thanksgiving." The words came out a bit harsher than she'd meant. And, once she said them, her throat tightened and tears shimmered under the surface.

He'd already turned away when she finally whispered, "There's a lot you don't know."

Come Sunday morning, Billy didn't seem to tire of yelling, "Time for church!"

The boys didn't need to be told twice. Joel, however, was made of sturdier stuff and rolled out of bed on the third call. Jared was already working somewhere outside. He had many different projects—all designed to keep theirs a working farm at a time when working farms were disappearing at an alarming rate.

The grim look on Billy's face could be interpreted two ways, Joel figured. First way, disappointment that yet again Jared was neglecting God. Second way, concern that Joel would step into a church while still lying about taking the money.

That Billy didn't immediately believe Joel's statement of innocence rankled Joel something fierce.

It also reminded him, yet again, that he'd stayed gone too long. Much of this was his own fault. As Beth had said, "family means more to others than it does to you. Always has."

Time to change that mind-set.

Dressed in his newest jeans and a clean but somewhat wrinkled plaid button-down shirt, Joel was about as spiffed up as he got.

On the drive to church, Joel noticed that during his absence, Roanoke had gotten spiffed up, too. The old dirt road that led to the church was gone, replaced by a blacktop on which Billy had to wait his turn—five vehicles were in front of him in the left-hand turn lane—before entering the church's parking lot.

"Even the ones who don't usually come are coming this morning," Billy remarked. "You're drawing more people than a door knocking."

Joel could already see people parking in the spill-over lot next to the church.

"I hope this means we're having a potluck," Ryan said from the backseat.

Great. By the time Billy found a space, Joel would be walking a mile—make that limping because he'd definitely overdone it yesterday—to the church's door. He'd gotten no sleep last night thanks to lower back pain, brought on not only from setting up a child's party but also from taking it down. Through the night his back sent message after painful message, time to relax, time to fill his prescriptions or soon he'd not be walking at all.

Ryan didn't need an answer. "Guess no potluck. None of these people are carrying plates." Of the three boys, Ryan looked to be the future football player and already knew his way around a full plate and how to get seconds before his little brothers had finished sneering at the green beans. "Hey, there's Brett!" Ryan continued, "Can I get out here and—"

"No," Joel said, picturing Ryan racing into the street and needing his uncle to race after him.

"No," Billy seconded. "We'll all arrive at the same time."

"I yike church," Caleb said happily.

"You yike everything," Matt grumbled. Little Caleb had been singing "Jesus Loves Me" the whole trip. Unfortunately, he didn't know all the words, so the first two verses had been repeated over and over.

Joel had reached for the minivan's radio, but Billy stopped him. "We don't need any more noise."

From the backseat, Matt was still grumping, "Do we have to go to church?"

It was a question Joel was already debating with himself. Over the years he'd been hit or miss at the cowboy churches, but his life always felt better during the hits.

Right now, he definitely needed life to feel better. But the church in Roanoke wasn't as easy to skip as the cowboy church. The Roanoke church actually *could* and *would* keep track of attendees and strays. And today, those people who hadn't attended Caleb's birthday party were, no doubt, primed and ready to see Joel.

"I can't be seen in a minivan," Joel had protested, wanting to postpone the inevitable.

"Why not?" Billy asked. "I'm seen in it just about every day. You better than me?"

"No," Joel sputtered, knowing he'd lost the one argument he'd never figured to have. Billy Staples in a minivan. Actually, it made sense.

Seemed Billy had been taking three rambunctious boys to church alone for quite some time, and now that he had someone to help with the kids, he didn't plan to let that someone escape.

Billy finally answered Matt's question, and his answer was aimed at everyone in the car. "You don't *have* to go to church. You *want* to go to church."

It was a page right out of the book of Mom. Joel's mom, Abigail McCreedy, had taken her two boys to church and let them know there was no place better to be. After their father died when Joel had just turned nine, if anything, she said it more often and meant it more for her than them.

"Look." Ryan pointed. "Matt, there's your teacher."

Everyone, even little Caleb, glanced over to where Beth Armstrong exited her two-door economy car. The wind picked up her golden hair and blew it around her face until she had to push it back and adjust the yellow headband that wasn't keeping a single strand in place. She wore bright red lipstick to church; she'd not worn any lipstick yesterday. Funny, Joel preferred her without it. She didn't need any help.

"I yike her," Caleb said.

"You don't know her," Ryan responded.

Joel waited to see what Matt would say, but the boy purposely avoided looking at his teacher. Joel couldn't seem to tear his eyes away. The wind was busy dancing with her yellow skirt.

He usually preferred his women in tight jeans, but maybe he'd been wrong all these years.

Beth's mother exited the passenger side, looking exactly the same as she had last Friday at the elementary school and exactly as she had a decade ago: somewhat unhappy.

"What were you and Beth talking about yesterday?" Billy asked. "I saw you coming back from the barn." It was a conversation Joel had half expected to have last night, but instead, once the party had ended and everything was cleaned up, Billy had taken his old truck and headed off somewhere.

Joel had spent the evening teaching Caleb Go Fish with Ryan's help. Matt had stayed on the couch drawing, only occasionally checking out what his brothers and uncle were doing.

Jared had come in from the field around eight—dirty, tired and hungry—and started to make himself a sandwich. Matt joined him, and soon Jared was making sandwiches for everyone except Joel.

Joel had taken that as his cue to head to bed.

Joel glanced back at Matt, but Matt's expression didn't change. He looked worried.

"We were talking about the family. How things change."

"*Harrumph.* That's not what I'd be talking about with someone as pretty as she is." Billy shook his head. "She's sure a smart one. Only one to listen to her mama and get a college degree. Wish you and your brother had listened to me."

"Hear that, boys." Joel twisted around—not a good idea—so he could see his nephews in the backseats. "Start planning now. Grandpa says you have to go to college." The expression on Billy's face said it all. Without college, it was either break your back or break your neck.

Since Joel represented the break-your-neck portion of the argument, he added, "I wish I'd gone to college."

"It's not too late," Billy said.

Before Joel could think on how to respond, Matt saved him. "She doesn't like me."

"Miss Armstrong likes everyone," Billy said.

"Not me," Matt muttered.

Or me, Joel thought. Yesterday, she'd all but stated that she thought his coming home only added to his brother's problems. And, when he had insisted he only wanted to help, she had rolled her eyes. Her parting words were, "You'll be gone before Thanksgiving."

He was of the opinion that she gave him that long because he needed time to heal. If she knew how much money he didn't have, she'd have given him until Christmas.

Billy finally pulled into the overflow lot and parked next to a truck even older than Joel's. Seemed Roanoke's church still had the same minister, who still drove the same truck. The minister's motto had been "waste not, want not." Joel could only hope the man's memory had some holes, because as Joel recalled the last time he'd spoken to Michael Russell, it had been to apologize for keeping his daughter out past curfew *and* for backing into his truck.

The minister's daughter had long ago married and moved to the big city of Des Moines. However, Joel noted as he crawled out of the minivan, the dent in the fender remained.

"Can I—" Ryan started.

"Go ahead," Billy said. "Catch up to your friend, but look out for cars in the parking lot."

Caleb stretched up his arms to be carried, and Joel grimaced when Billy picked up the little thirty-pounder.

Billy didn't need to be carting Caleb around so much, not when Joel could help. He also needed a job so he could pay his brother rent. He'd been thinking about striking out on his own once he got back on his feet, but last night had shown him that maybe, just maybe, he was needed.

Not by Jared, nope, his big brother made that perfectly clear, but by Billy and his nephews.

Especially the one dragging his feet as they neared the front of the church building. Matt came to a complete standstill once they reached the walk.

Oh, oh. Beth Armstrong waited by the entryway. Her smile was Iowa sunshine graced by the green grass of her eyes. If he'd had a hat on, Joel would be removing it. At least that would give him something to do since he couldn't think of a word to say. Even if he had thought of a word, it wouldn't make it past his tongue.

"Matt, it's good to see you. You're in time to help me set up the room for Bible class."

"Now that I have Joel's assistance," Billy said, "we should be on time more often."

Her eyes really weren't forest green. They were chilly green diamonds and right now they sent out a cold message predicting that Billy would be back on his own soon.

"Good to hear," she said, but Joel knew she wasn't

thinking it. She held out her hand, but Matt didn't move to take it. Instead, he looked down at his feet.

"Go ahead, son," Billy encouraged.

"I used to help my Bible school teacher," Joel said, his words sounding a bit raspy. "It's fun."

Matt looked up and looked at Joel accusingly. "Then you come with me."

Chapter Six

Watching Joel McCreedy slowly take the chairs from atop the Bible school tables and sit them on the floor reminded Beth of something she'd forgotten.

The man truly was wounded, not just from the rodeo, but also from the accident last Thursday evening.

The Joel she remembered had a flair most cowboys didn't. He'd have had those chairs on the floor in a minute without much noise and fanfare. Now, when he lifted and bent, he reminded her a little of Grandpa Billy, who'd come in the classroom more than once to encourage Matt. Come to think of it, Joel sounded a bit like Billy, too, every time he let out his breath.

She'd have offered to help him, but he'd have only moved faster to prove he didn't need help.

He wouldn't appreciate her comparing him to Grandpa Billy, either, at least not when it came to how slow he was moving.

Matt sat in a chair, crossed his arms and stared at the speckled brown-and-black carpeting as Joel and Beth did the work he was supposed to be helping with.

"When I was in this class," Joel said, straightening to his full height and making the room suddenly look small, "I got in trouble for running in the room and jumping on the table."

Beth sincerely doubted it was the same table.

Matt looked up for a nanosecond and managed to look a little interested.

"Then," Joel continued, "I slid right across the top and landed on the floor."

Matt studied the table as if measuring how much of a slide and how deep a fall.

"I wasn't his teacher," Beth informed Matt, her eyes casting a halfhearted warning. "I'd never allow that."

"Oh, the kindergarten teacher back then didn't allow it, either. I often got a good talking to out back."

Now Matt was watching Joel instead of the carpeting. Maybe telling tales of mischief was not what all the teaching books suggested, but it might be what worked. Not only was Joel taking a break he obviously needed, but Matt looked more intrigued than Beth had seen him all year.

Without looking at Matt, because that would have given the ploy away, Beth said, "What else did you do?"

"The classrooms were pretty limiting," Joel admitted. He looked at one of the walls. It had a large mural painted on it of children singing. "The most we had on the wall were attendance charts."

"I painted that," Beth admitted.

"Impressive," Joel said. Then he looked back at Matt. "I think the time Jared and I accidentally threw a tennis ball in the baptistery was probably the most interesting."

Beth raised an eyebrow. "What were you doing near the baptistery with a tennis ball?"

Joel chuckled, getting some color back now that he'd stopped fiddling with the chairs. "It was a workday. I was probably about Matt's age, and Jared was Ryan's age. Mom was in the nursery helping paint the walls. My dad was doing something to a pipe. I don't remember what. Jared and I were supposed to be in the overflow watching a movie with the other kids, but we'd already seen it."

The mention of his dad's name inspired Matt to forget that he was feigning disinterest.

"Jared found the tennis ball, and we were kicking it down the hallway and into the foyer. We heard Dad laughing and headed his way, thinking we'd just see what he was doing. We'd barely opened the door when we heard the minister behind us."

"The same minister we have now?" Matt asked.

"Oh, yes," Joel said ominously. "Jared started to run, changed his mind and then started to run again. His foot hit the ball and away it flew. Looked just like a tiny soccer ball arcing for a goal. Plop, right into the baptistery."

Matt's eyes got big. "Did Daddy get in trouble?"

"You know," Joel said slowly, "we didn't. The minister poked his head in the auditorium, asked what was going on, and when Dad said he had it under control, the minister left. Then Dad got a pair of waders on, fetched the ball and told us to go play outside. Jared and I couldn't believe our luck. Of course, he didn't give us the ball back."

Beth watched as Joel's eyes sobered. Like her, he'd lost his father at a fairly young age; unlike her, his mother had remarried after a few years.

"Your father loved you very much," Beth said softly. She didn't remember her father at all. By the time she'd been born, he'd started making a name for himself as a rock climber. He'd died, from a fall, when she was three. "How old were you, when he…?"

He knew exactly what she was asking. "Nine."

"Old enough to remember," she said softly.

"Did you ever get in trouble?" Matt asked. Beth started. He was looking at her instead of the ground, and for the first time, he actually looked interested in what she might have to say.

"No, I really didn't get in much trouble. I did do something funny once, here at church. As a matter of fact—" she looked at Matt "—your dad even got involved."

Matt's eyes grew big; Joel's did, too.

Well, she'd been the one to bring it up, so now she had to go on. "It's not nearly so daring a story as the ones your uncle Joel has been sharing with you." She sent Joel an exaggerated scowl of disapproval. "When I was in second grade, my sister Linda accused me of chewing used gum from the bottom of the pew."

"Ew." Matt made a face.

"Exactly how I felt," Beth agreed. "I hadn't been chewing gum from the bottom of the pew, and I had no idea what she was talking about. One Sunday we got here early. I forget why, and I went into the auditorium and crawled under the pew where I'd been sitting when Linda accused me of chewing somebody else's gum. I wanted to see if there really was gum down there."

"And?" Matt questioned.

"Linda was right. I counted five wads of used chewing gum under my spot."

"There's ten wads of gum there now," Joel predicted.

"No." Matt's eyes were as big as saucers.

"How was my brother involved? That's what I want to know," Joel said.

"He came into the auditorium and saw me under the pew and asked what I was doing. When I told him, he said he figured there were at least a thousand wads of gum under all the pews."

"You think he was right?" Matt asked.

"Not back then," Beth said, "but maybe today. Jared took one half of the church and I took the other. I don't remember how many we counted, but it wasn't a thousand."

"My dad actually crawled under the pews and counted old bubble gum?" Matt clearly didn't believe it.

"Not only that," Beth said, "but he also showed me where he usually sat and took credit for some wads."

"That's probably why I'm not allowed to chew gum in church or anywhere," Matt said sorrowfully.

Before any more secrets could be shared, a low chime sounded.

"Shouldn't there be kids here by now?" Joel asked as Matt jumped up and headed out the door mumbling something about making sure he got a chocolate one.

"We've been trying something new for the last two years," Beth said. "Instead of classes starting right at ten, we meet in the overflow room and have coffee and doughnuts. It's a good time to greet one another before we jump right into lessons."

Falling in step beside her as she exited the room, Joel raised an eyebrow.

"It's also," Beth continued, "supposed to help the classes start without so many stragglers."

"Is it working?"

"Not a bit."

"Looks like everyone's on time today," Joel said.

No surprise, in true small-town fashion, everyone had turned out to see the return of the prodigal son. And since the party Billy had thrown happened to be a birthday party for a three-year-old instead of a welcome-home-prodigal party, they'd instead traveled to church to see Joel.

"How many of these people believe I stole the school's Rodeo Club money?" Joel asked out of the side of his mouth.

Beth was surprised. He seemed so nonchalant, not even mentioning the money to her during their few talks.

And she certainly never intended to bring it up.

Who knew what was going through his mind? Certainly, not her. He'd been in Roanoke only four days and their paths had crossed on each and every one. Yet, all they'd done was dance around formalities.

He let it be known he was attracted. Only a rogue would manage so much in just four days.

She let it be known she wasn't attracted. He obviously saw through the ruse.

What was a surprise was Joel's downplaying of his welcome. Instead of basking in the attention, he looked somewhat humble as he nodded and gave a brief wave of greeting.

"The minister will appreciate the crowd," Beth offered.

And it was a crowd. She couldn't remember the

last time she'd seen the room this full. Every seat was taken, and judging by the empty serving plates and Matt's disappointed expression, they'd missed all the doughnuts.

Another chime sounded, and everyone but Joel seemed to know what to do. The kids scampered off to class and the adults followed. Beth gave his shoulder a comforting pat like she might a schoolboy and headed for her classroom. Her perfume lingered.

Left to his own wanderings, it crossed Joel's mind to help those who were beginning to clean up the kitchen and tables, but he was already moving slower than usual, and he'd rather save his strength for later. Besides, he wasn't ready to answer questions.

Time to reacquaint himself with the old church. At one time, it had been a second home. At first glance, it looked the same, only smaller.

The main door opened to a short hallway. To the left was a classroom and the restrooms. The preacher's office was to the right. Joel had been in there two times. Once to discuss getting baptized; the next to explain why he'd accidentally kept the preacher's daughter out after curfew and the damage he'd done to the minister's car.

The minister liked books and his room had been overflowing with them. Strangely enough, the minister also liked bull riding and had even engaged in the sport. He'd never earned a buckle or a purse, but he had a photo proudly displayed. The minister hadn't made his eight seconds, and the picture showed the man somewhat above the bull instead of on it.

Joel had never been brave enough to ask about that ride.

The main door opened, a couple—both looking just a few years older than Joel—hurried in and paused as they walked past him. Obviously they knew where to go. They greeted him with "Good to have you with us today" and "Stick around after services, you'll find us a real friendly bunch."

"I'm Joel Mc—"

They headed down the stairs and to Bible class before Joel got more than his first name out. They were worried about being late. He was more worried about being accepted.

Imagine being mistaken for a stranger in the church his grandfather had helped build.

At the end of the hall was a square-shaped lobby. The perfect size for fellowship. People staying after services to talk could be privy to the conversations taking place around them. Like when—unable to wait for the noon dinner he'd planned—Jared had proposed to Mandy in this lobby, amid a crowd of people. There'd been applause, and Jared had looked happy. Later, no one remembered if Mandy had said yes or not.

Then again, people rarely said no to Jared.

In the lobby, one wall held photos of the church members, plus there was a door that led to the basement, where most of the classes were. Two other walls held the coatracks. In late September, only a few sweaters claimed the hangers. In winter, the racks would be full of coats and scarves. Dark boots would muddy the carpeting below. The final wall held a display of tracts as well as the opening to the main auditorium, where the adults' Bible study class was held.

Joel walked through the opening and slipped into the last pew, toward the wall and away from the main aisle and the other worshippers.

He almost stood back up. The last time he'd sat here, same pew, was at his mother's funeral.

In the end, it was his mother's memory that kept him in the pew. How disappointed she'd be to know how many Sundays he'd not sat in a pew or on a bench at cowboy church.

Or on his knees in prayer.

The voice of the teacher droned on. Joel was tuned in to the deep alto but didn't comprehend the words. He'd judged his brother for missing church today, but Joel was just as guilty, sitting here in church but not really listening to a word. There was a scripture. Joel had no clue from which book in the Bible, but he remembered the verse in its entirety. *"Why do you look at the speck of sawdust in your brother's eye and pay no attention to the plank in your own eye?"*

Joel had so much to atone for.

For one thing, he'd spent the last eight years only thinking about number one. He'd been aware of his selfishness, but he'd kept thinking he had time: time to get one more purse, one more belt, make it to Vegas and the world championship, make it to number one.

In truth, Joel had made himself his first priority.

With that kind of attitude, why should he be surprised when his brother didn't welcome him back with open arms…? Why should he be surprised when Billy didn't immediately believe that Joel hadn't stolen the RC money?

Today was a good day to start changing, start mending fences and focusing on other people instead of himself. Joel closed his eyes, bowed his head and said a quick prayer. He was trying for heartfelt but actually was more relieved when he finally opened his eyes. Observing the auditorium, he could see the good people of the congregation looking out for one another instead of only for themselves.

As the Sunday school lesson came to an end, the minister's eyes settled on Joel with no readable expression. Joel could only guess what the man was thinking. Maybe he was worrying about the condition of his truck out in the parking lot. Maybe he was thinking about the daughter Joel had dated back when they were freshmen in high school. Maybe he was thinking about changing the sermon to something about thieves. Maybe he was thinking about the gum under the pews.

Maybe, just maybe, he was relieved to see Joel returning to the flock.

Once more a chime sounded, followed by the noise of doors opening and closing. Footsteps clamored up the stairs and soon the young people who'd attended their own Bible school shuffled in. Then, too, there were those people who just came for the main service.

Billy walked in and made his way up front before sitting down next to a woman Joel didn't know. The woman immediately leaned over and whispered something in Billy's ear. After a moment, Billy nodded.

Joel's one-time best friend, Derek, and his wife were headed for the middle section of the church. Brittney, Derek's wife, held a tiny baby against her shoulder. A cap graced the little girl's head. After settling them in, Derek took his daughter, cupping the baby's head ever so gently.

The McClanahans, the two oldest generations, were in attendance. He owed them a new portion of fence.

He'd forgotten.

What he'd also forgotten was the crescendo of a church's auditorium as people flocked together—the sound of friendships, laughter and living.

Joel found Beth's sisters. He hadn't noticed them at first although they'd been there during the Bible hour. Susan looked like she had swallowed a balloon. Linda, on the other hand, had turned into a sleek fashion model. Her graceful neck swiveled to the left and to the right as she perused the room. When she saw Joel, she smiled—a Cheshire cat smile, one he recognized from high school. Back then, it had meant she had some grand plan that she shouldn't act on, one that she was sure had a positive side. He doubted she'd changed much, on the inside.

The first time attending a brick-and-mortar congregation in many years, you'd think he would pay rapt attention.

Joel didn't.

The ghosts of his past kept tapping him on the shoulder. Thing was, some of the memories made him uncomfortable, made him feel both guilty yet melancholy at the same time as if there were memories just out of reach, things he should be thinking, doing, *knowing*.

He shouldn't have stayed gone. He should have paid more attention to what was left of his family. He should have been busy making more memories.

Here.

As if to emphasize what he'd been missing, Beth Armstrong, all prim and proper, walked into the auditorium and started down the aisle toward her sisters.

She did what no one else had.

She looked right at Joel.

Then, Miss Prim and Proper winked.

Chapter Seven

❧

"This is a waste of money. I could have easily prepared a meal and had it waiting." Patsy Armstrong rarely enjoyed eating at restaurants, a fact her children knew well.

They also knew that if they ate lunch after church at her house, they'd need to stay the whole afternoon or hear about it.

"I know, Mother," Susan said. "But I was craving fried chicken."

The one dish Mom had never mastered.

Her lips pursed together, just for a moment, and then she seemed to shake it off. "Understandable," she allowed. After all, her middle daughter's pregnancy cravings couldn't be ignored.

Susan's husband, Alex, helped get his wife comfortable. He was on patrol today, but this was his lunch hour. He was well aware what his mother-in-law thought of his profession. Beth had to admit, he took it in stride, rarely letting Mom's snide remarks about the dangers of his job hit their target.

"So," said Patsy after they were all settled in, "what do you think of the new fifth grade teacher?"

Around the table, Beth's sisters relaxed. The topic of the day would be the state of Beth's life instead of theirs.

"He seems very nice," Beth answered. "He just moved here from Hawaii and—"

"Why would anyone willingly leave Hawaii?" Linda wanted to know. "And then move here?"

"Iowa, and especially Roanoke, is a great place to live," Patsy said indignantly. "He sounds like a smart young man."

The waitress showed up then, putting water glasses on the table and passing out menus.

Linda didn't even open her menu, she pushed it away. She'd order a hamburger and fries. She always did. Then, she'd laugh at both Susan and Beth as they complained about how she never gained a pound. She was laughing now, laughing at Beth as she teased, "I agree with Mom. I think this fifth grade teacher sounds pretty good. He'll probably need to fly back to Hawaii occasionally for family stuff. And you, of course, little Beth, will take along a sister or two."

"And niece," Susan said, patting her stomach. Her menu joined Linda's. She'd be ordering fried chicken whether she craved it or not.

"Nephew," Alex contradicted.

Even Beth had to smile. Her older sisters amazed her. They had something she'd always wanted: the ability to be spontaneous and the ability to enjoy almost any venue.

"I wouldn't start saving my pennies yet," Beth said after the waitress took their order. "He moved here because his brother works in Bettendorf. Apparently, they're close. Plus, he's flying home at Christmas to marry his girlfriend."

Mom shook her head.

"You know," Susan said, "there are plenty of available men here in Roanoke."

Mom looked interested; Beth suddenly felt afraid.

"We have a new guy starting next week," Alex offered. "I haven't met him yet, but I know he's single. He's the right age, too."

Susan elbowed him.

"One cop is quite enough," Mom said.

"I'm interested," Linda said quickly.

It was only the beginning of the meal, which meant Beth still had at least an hour to suffer. No chance would Linda be able to divert attention to her. Mom was on a mission and today Beth was the target.

"There's the new doctor," Susan said.

"Oh." Mom leaned forward. "I've met him. Nice, nice man although I've not seen him at church. Maybe he goes to the Oak Street congregation. I'll have to ask Peg."

"I'm interested, too," Linda said again. Without

thinking, she turned to Beth and said, "Did you meet him the other night? I hear he's cute."

"I didn't notice." Luckily the part about Beth possibly meeting the new doctor sidetracked Beth's mom from thinking about why Beth had encountered the man.

The waitress came with their salads, but Beth had lost her appetite. She knew exactly what her mother was doing and why. Ever since Mom discovered that Beth not only had witnessed Joel's accident, but had taken him to the hospital and then *stayed,* Mom had grabbed every opportunity to list all the reasons why someone like Joel McCreedy should be avoided.

As if to prove Mom was right, the door to the restaurant opened and in walked Joel and his family, except for Jared. Matt saw her right away, ducked his head and tried to hide behind Billy.

"What have you done to the kid?" Linda whispered.

"Nothing, he's just shy."

Joel, however, wasn't shy. His face lit up. For a moment it looked like he'd be heading their way, but then the hostess said something to Billy and soon the men were heading for a table on the other side of the room.

Susan practically stood up to get a better view. "Wow, Joel looks great."

"Sit down," Mom hissed. "We don't want him to think we're interested in anything he has to say."

"I'm interested," Susan said. "I've not seen him since graduation. Alex, you've never even met him, right?"

"Right," Alex agreed, "but I've certainly heard of him."

Suddenly having a police officer as a son-in-law no longer seemed to bother Mom. "Have you heard anything lately?"

"Only from my wife and you."

"Me?" Mom said indignantly. "I haven't said anything."

"Uh," Susan admitted, "I told him about your little confrontation with Joel on Friday when he came to pick up his nephews."

Beth felt her throat tighten. Tomorrow she'd have to avoid the teacher's lounge because no doubt Mom's actions would be the chief topic.

"He didn't come to pick up his nephews. He came because he needed Mr. Staples to give him a ride home."

"She's right," Joel said, standing behind Beth's chair and gripping the backrest. "I needed a ride home. It's going to take a while before Tiny can get the part for my truck. Good to see everybody. Susan, you look fabulous."

Beth could feel the side of his hand brushing against her shoulder. There was no reason for her to feel warmth spreading through her body. He wasn't touching her on purpose.

Or was he?

Next time she winked at a man in church, she'd make sure her mother wasn't around to see the backlash!

"I can't believe you still have that old truck," Susan said. "It's older than you are."

"Actually," Joel admitted, "it's older than you and me combined."

Beth stayed out of the banter, half of her wishing she knew how to engage in such easy conversation and the other half focused on her mother's face. Patsy had turned a queer shade of pale, and her lips were practically nonexistent. Her hands were folded in her lap.

This wasn't just about Joel's taking money that didn't belong to him. No, there was something else. But what? Quickly Beth looked at her sisters. They'd each hung around with Joel. Linda'd even called him her boyfriend for a week or two during high school. But Linda had called just about every boy in Roanoke her boyfriend at one time or another.

"Hi, Miss Armstrong." Matt joined them, appearing too solemn in his church clothes. "Grandpa said I needed to come over here."

"It's good to see you again," Beth said. "Did you tell your grandpa what you learned in Bible class?"

"Uh, no."

"Grandpa suggested that I not come over here," Joel said, looking right at Beth. "But I'm willing to tell you what I learned in Bible class."

"I think our food's about to arrive," Mom said.

"Let's take the hint," Joel said, reaching for Matt's hand. "Good seeing you all." He led Matt back to their table. Beth couldn't help it. She twisted in her seat so she could watch Joel's every move. As if sensing her eyes, Joel turned around.

Beth was well aware that her mother was watching Joel's every move. Joel knew it, too.

He winked.

Even above the noise of the waitress setting out their plates, Beth could hear the suppressed giggles of her sisters, as well as her mother's muted disapproving gasp. Thankfully, they couldn't see Beth's face, because if they could, they'd know she was a goner.

Her sisters would tease her unmercifully. As for her mother...

Beth looked across at her sister Susan and remembered something she'd said when it became apparent that Alex was the one. "I can't pick the man I'm going to spend the next sixty years with based on Mom's criteria."

Made sense, and maybe it was the fear of both meeting and not meeting Mom's criteria that kept Beth from enjoying the few dates she'd had. Still, right now, Joel was the last person on earth who Beth needed to be attracted to. Not only was he in Roanoke for a temporary stay, but as a bull rider and possible thief, he also topped her mother's list of unsuitable men.

Beth shouldn't have winked at him this morning at church. It was just that her morning had gone perfectly from the time she had arrived at the church to the time she had walked into the worship service, and seeing Joel there had made her happy.

Her wink told him more than he needed to know.

She wasn't sure what she was feeling at this moment, but she suspected that the only reason it wasn't happiness had to do with the stoic, somewhat white-faced woman sitting next to her. Beth had spent most of her life trying to please her mother.

What Beth felt now couldn't possibly please her mother.

But Beth couldn't remember the last time she'd winked at a member of the opposite sex who was over the age of six.

"Well," Billy said when Joel got back to the table, "did Patsy tell you to get lost?"

"She didn't say anything," Matt said, sounding more animated than Joel had ever heard. "But she looked at Joel just like you look at Daddy when he beats you at checkers."

"I couldn't have described it better," Joel told Matt.

Billy started to grin, but then noticed Joel's face. "It's been a while since I've lost a good game of checkers. You were always a worthy opponent. We'll have to play."

Joel nodded, his mind on the table across the dining room. He wondered if Beth Armstrong knew what a fire she'd ignited. Because right now, Joel wasn't thinking about physical therapy. He wasn't thinking about the ride.

He was thinking about a female.

Not a good idea since he'd be staying in Roanoke such a limited time.

There really wasn't much time to dwell on Beth. Joel wasn't sure if he appreciated or regretted the distraction of eating a meal at a restaurant with three young boys.

He needed to decide whether he wanted to engage or retreat in the game of Beth Armstrong.

But first Joel needed to get through lunch. Ryan decided right away what he wanted off the menu and was irritated that he had to wait while Matt looked at every single lunch option available. As for Caleb, his favorite meal morning, noon and night was peanut butter and jelly. A meal the restaurant didn't have.

"We usually get him chicken strips," Billy explained, "because someday there will be a breakthrough and he'll develop his taste buds."

Billy finally ordered meals for both Matt and Caleb. Matt sulked and Caleb didn't care. Joel soon found out why. The moment the food arrived, Caleb lost interest in the toy car he was playing with and started squirming.

"We took too long ordering," Billy said. "We have about a twenty-minute window with him. That's how long he'll sit still. I'll take him for a walk while you eat. Then, you walk with him while I eat."

"That's what Mom and Dad used to do," Ryan said, "with Matt."

"You eat first," Joel suggested to Billy. "I'm not all that hungry."

It was during their third trip around the restaurant, with Caleb dividing his time between running through the grass or balancing on the sidewalk's curb, that Beth walked out the front door.

Caleb ran right to her. "Miss Beth. Miss Beth. I'm still three."

She didn't miss a beat. "And I'm still Miss Beth."

"Unca Joel is walking with me. You can come?"

"No, but thank you for the offer. I need to be heading home. I've got some things to do."

"Go ahead, walk with us," Joel invited. "I'll use the time to ask you out again and to thank you for saving my life."

"I didn't save your life. You'd have regained consciousness and driven yourself to the hospital."

"No, I wouldn't have. I needed you."

"Well, you've said thank-you already. That's enough." She checked her watch. "I need to be going."

"You're right," Joel jumped in. "Going out with me? Tonight? Dinner?"

"Joel, you'll be here for a few months and then you'll leave." She was speaking to him, but not looking at him. Instead, she was peering into the restaurant with a resigned look on her face. Joel came, stood next to her and peered into the dining room.

Patsy Armstrong stared back at them.

"You've always been really good at leaving people behind," Beth said, tussling Caleb's hair and heading for her car.

"You take every opportunity to throw that in my face. Maybe I never knew they cared."

It was too late. She was out of hearing range.

Caleb tugged on Joel's pant leg. "I care."

Chapter Eight

"You wanna tell me what really happened?"

More than anything, Joel wanted to tell his friend Max what had happened to the mangled fence. Instead, he had Max's seventy-something father—who was also a Max—informing Joel how he should have been over yesterday fixing his fence, not helping with a three-year-old's birthday party.

Joel felt like he was sixteen again. He also knew this conversation wasn't going to end with Mr. McClanahan feeling any differently about Joel.

"Mr. McClanahan, I fell asleep at the wheel."

Max raised an eyebrow.

"Really. I'd been on the road all day Thursday, and—" Joel didn't want to talk to Max about being turned away by Jared. Max was an elder at the church and probably of the same mind as Billy when it came to helping family members "—I should have pulled over, but I didn't."

The older man's eyebrow remained raised but he

didn't press. "I have plenty of wire in the shed out behind the barn. You do remember how to make a post?"

"I remember."

"Then I'm expecting this fence back in shape before the week is out."

Joel didn't tell Max about his injury or his need for physical therapy.

Later that evening, after Sunday-night services, when he and Billy sat at the kitchen table with a checkerboard, he told Billy. To his surprise, Billy laughed and said, "You know that Todd Lehman retired a few years ago."

Lehman had been the physical therapist who'd come to the high school and worked with the football players. Joel wasn't surprised to hear he'd retired. He'd been aged back then.

"Well," Billy continued, "I don't think I saw you with him tonight, but I definitely saw you talking to the new physical therapist this morning at church."

"Who?"

"Nathan Fisher."

"The youth minister?"

"That's his passion. His physical therapy practice is what pays his bills."

Joel half expected a sermon to follow. Billy had always been big on not being a burden and having a solid career.

"You still able to pay your bills?" Billy asked, taking control of the game and quickly taking two of Joel's pieces.

Joel didn't answer, which Billy correctly guessed as a no.

"Then," Billy said, "you're going to have to work while you're home."

Home. Just the word made Joel feel a little better. To celebrate the feeling, he took one of Billy's pieces.

"Best thing you can do," Billy advised, "is take over manning Solitaire's Market on the weekends. It's only open until the end of October. That would free Jared up some to spend time with his children."

"You think he'd let me?"

Billy pursed his lips and didn't answer for a few moments. "I can arrange it." He took another one of Joel's pieces. "How much money do you have?"

"Two dollars and thirty cents."

Billy looked startled. "What were you thinking you'd do about therapy?"

"I wasn't thinking past getting home and resting a couple days so I could get the energy to come up with a game plan." Joel took another piece and earned a crown.

"Well, for now," Billy said, "how about our game plan be that you work around here? I'll loan you a couple hundred until you get on your feet. Plus, I'll talk to Nathan and start a payment plan for the physical therapy. Good enough?"

Joel shook his head. "I'll work at the market, and

I'll take the offer for physical therapy, but I don't need a loan."

He did need the loan, actually, but just the thought of taking it made him feel like he was on the edge of a very high cliff and about to fall off.

Solitaire's Market actually was a good idea, if Jared went for it. Joel would only need to work weekends. The rest of the time, he could be working on strengthening his back, and he could also be working on getting Beth to agree to dinner.

It was good to be home.

Billy half frowned, half smiled a moment later when Joel took control of the board with three crowned pieces.

The game finally ended. Joel looked across the table at his stepfather.

Billy Staples was a good foot shorter than his two stepsons. His hair was thin and gray. Yet he always stood tall. Jared and Joel had spent a lost two years after their real father died. When their mother remarried, she'd picked a winner. Billy had come in and instead of saying, "I'm here now," he showed it. He sat down and helped with their homework. He drove them to football games and stayed to watch in the bleachers. When they got hurt, he either doctored them himself or hauled them to the hospital. He made their mother smile again.

Even eight years after her death, he was helping the next generation with their homework and still doing doctor duty.

"I'm sorry," Joel said.

Both men knew he wasn't talking about winning the checkers game.

The following Friday, the whir of the tractor and the sounds of snickering woke him up again. This time, he didn't feel like a horse had stepped on his head and galloped over his back or that he'd attempted to swallow a cup of sawdust.

"Grandpa Billy says you're taking us to school," Ryan said.

"I get to go, too," Caleb added. "Cuz Grandpa has tings to do."

Joel opened one eye and glared at his nephews.

They didn't notice. He'd been there just over a week, and now they figured he belonged to them: Caleb and Ryan, that is.

"Grandpa says if you don't get up, you don't get breakfast," Ryan added.

For some reason, Joel felt hungrier than he'd felt for months, maybe years. Must be all the work he'd been doing, carefully doing, around their farm and the McClanahan farm. Except for mending the McClanahans' fence, he'd been doing mostly inside stuff. Over the last week, he'd put in a new garbage disposal; seemed they'd gone without a working one for two years. Then he installed a new ceiling fan in the living room. According to Billy, the old one had never worked right. He'd also gone into Jared's territory, the master bedroom, and made it so the toilet in there flushed quicker.

He didn't get a thanks.

After that, Joel moved outside, where he worked on the ATV Jared sometimes used to get from one end of the farm to the other in a hurry.

He had nothing on his agenda today except to sleep.

Seemed his nephews and stepfather had other ideas. He carefully rolled off the bed and raised his arms, twisting his fingers into claws. "Grrrooowwwlll."

Caleb ran from the room, squealing in delight. Ryan took a step back, his grin mischievous. He enjoyed games.

Only Matt, who'd come as far as the hallway outside the guest room door, truly looked scared.

"Just kidding," Joel said lamely.

"We know that," Ryan said. "Come on, Matt. Let's tell Grandpa the monster is on his way."

Joel quickly dressed. Matt might be the brother who thought of others first, but Ryan definitely was willing to step up to the plate if needed.

There were five plates on the table. The spot that had belonged to Mandy wasn't set. Billy made quick work of dishing out pancakes and eggs and pouring milk.

"I like being taken care of," Joel said, downing half his milk in one gulp.

"Me, too," Ryan said. He watched what Joel was

doing and tried to drink half of his own milk. He succeeded in three medium gulps: two that made it to his stomach and one that stayed on his chin.

"I like being taken care of, too," Billy said, handing Ryan another napkin. "I need you to take the boys to school. Don't forget to stop by the McClanahan place and pick up Trey."

"I can do that," Joel agreed. Taking the boys to school meant the chance to bump accidentally on purpose into Beth. He'd tried to find her Wednesday night at midweek church services but she'd apparently arrived late and then hadn't stuck around.

"Caleb, too," Billy added.

"An almost perfect plan," Joel said. "Except I'm going to start physical therapy, hopefully this morning, so what should I do with Caleb?"

For a moment, he thought Billy wanted to shrug. Instead, his stepfather went to a drawer and pulled out an address book. Flipping to a page, he showed Joel a place called Ducky's Day Care. "In a pinch, we leave Caleb there. Usually, if I have more time, we can find someone from church or a neighbor, but this is a little last minute."

Joel recognized the street address. "Can I leave him there long enough to head to Tiny's and see what he thinks about the truck?"

"That's up to you. Caleb can stay at Ducky's. I just need you to be home in time for lunch, so be here at straight up noon," Billy said. "I have something to talk to both you and Jared about."

"What?"

"I'll let you know when you're both together."

Something didn't feel right, but Joel knew better than to push. Billy wasn't about to say anything until both brothers were around. A half hour later, Joel had finished eating, gotten dressed and had the boys loaded in the van and was on his way to Max's.

In a minivan!

Even Max chuckled as he opened the rear door and ushered Trey into the backseat before coming over to Joel's rolled-down window. "How the mighty have fallen."

"Temporarily," Joel replied. In a few words, he filled Max in on the back injury. Roanoke didn't hold secrets well and since Joel would start therapy today, he might as well set the record straight. "The therapist I saw back in New Mexico said six months, but I'm hoping that what I do here moves it up to Christmas."

"That's probably pushing it, but you've always been willing to take chances," Max said.

Joel thought of Beth. "And I intend to continue doing so."

"Uncle Joel, we're going to be late," Matt said. "I hate being late."

"I don't mind being late," said Ryan.

"I'm three," Caleb told Trey.

"I'm twenty-six," Max told Caleb, "same as your uncle."

"Wow," was Caleb's response.

"It's good to have you back," Max told Joel. "Your brother needs all the help he can get."

Joel mentally supplied what Max didn't say... "since Mandy's death."

But Max finished with something completely different. "He's missed you."

"We're going to be late," Matt said again.

"You don't even know how to tell time," Ryan complained.

"No," Matt said, "but I know how long we stay here when Grandpa picks Trey up and this is a lot longer."

"Grandpa's not seeing a friend he hasn't seen in years," Joel protested.

"Not our fault," Matt grumbled.

"You had good reason to stay away," Max said.

"Rodeoing," Joel stated firmly. "Back then, I wanted to make it to Nationals and win." He looked at Max, trying to read his friend's expression. It was somewhat wary. So, Joel pressed on. "Rodeoing wasn't the only reason I stayed away. I also stayed away so that Jared and Mandy had time and space."

Max nodded.

"I've heard about the RC money," Joel said, lowering his voice. For some reason, he didn't want the boys to overhear, but they already knew. Ryan had brought it up last Friday. A little louder, he proclaimed, "Believe me, I didn't take it."

"I never thought you did," Max said.

If that were true, Joel thought, there'd be no need for relief to fill his best friend's face.

"I'll find out who did take it," Joel promised, "and set me up."

"We lose points if we're tardy," Matt said.

Suddenly, Ryan took notice. "And we have to make up the time during afternoon recess."

"As you can see," Joel said drily, "I'm more chauffeur than uncle and I'm not doing my job."

Max grinned. "Get used to it. With kids, there's always something."

The boys were not late to school. Obviously, Billy liked to get them to school the moment the playground opened and a teacher was on duty. Now, after finding a parking place in a sea of trucks and minivans and parents hurrying their offspring along, Joel was at a loss.

"Trey and I know what to do." Ryan saved the day. "But Grandpa still makes sure Matt gets to the playground and puts his backpack in the right place."

"Can't you do that?" Joel asked.

Ryan thought about it for a minute. "Maybe, but Matt's still a little scar—"

"No, I'm not." To prove it, Matt started undoing his seat belt and climbing over Trey to make it to the door.

"I yike walking Matt to class," Caleb announced.

"Then that's what we'll do."

Four boys and one man spilled out of the minivan. Ryan and Trey walked ahead, leading the way, but Joel knew it well. A good twenty years ago, his mother had held his hand when he was in kindergarten, as they followed a swaggering Jared to the very same playground.

The school was bigger, thanks to a renovation, but the beige color on the hallway walls was the same. The bulletin board decorations and the names of the teachers were both different and the same.

Beth was walking the playground, bending down to say something to a little girl and then blowing a sharp whistle at a boy who was walking on top of the monkey bars instead of swinging from them. The morning wind momentarily sent her hair whipping across her face, blinding her, but she recovered and took two steps toward the monkey-bar offender. He jumped down.

The back of Joel's neck prickled. He turned and saw Beth's mother. She was carrying a stack of paper and walking toward him.

"Mr. McCreedy, if you're going to be picking up your nephews, you'll need to have Jared fill out the correct forms. If not, I can't release—"

He nodded, uttered a "yes, ma'am" and retreated. If he intended to win over Beth, he'd need to win over her mother first, and that would take time and planning.

Ducky's Day Care was only three minutes away and luckily, Caleb liked going there. Joel entered, introduced himself to the woman in charge, whom he remembered from school, and headed for physical therapy.

After an hour and a half of light sit-ups, followed by a hot wrap, Joel headed back to the farm. He arrived just before noon and entered a quiet house.

"Billy!" A quick perusal through all the rooms didn't help. Joel went to the back door and stepped outside to look toward the cornfield.

There, it wasn't so quiet. Joel could see the puff from Jared's tractor and hear it as it neared the barn. When it shut off, the silence seemed almost accusatory. Sure, there were the sound of birds and a distant moan from one of the cows, but background noise didn't count. Joel turned, entered the house and walked to the front yard.

No sign of Billy.

Funny, Joel thought, stepping into the living room and listening to the sound of Jared's boots coming up the porch stairs and then into the house. *It's been a long time since I've been home alone with just my brother.* There'd always been someone around, be it Billy or Mandy.

"Why are you just standing there?" Jared asked.

Sweat stained the front and sides of his shirt. A smudge of dirt was above his left cheek. Joel took a good hard look at his older brother and didn't like what he saw. Jared had aged, and the chip on his shoulder had doubled in size.

"I was waiting for you."

"Where's Billy?"

"I was hoping you'd know."

"He said if I wanted lunch to make sure I headed back at noon. It's four after. I'm hungry." Jared headed for the kitchen. His boots pounded angrily on the paneled floor. Joel followed, aware that he was trying not to let his boots make noise, as if the sound would offend his brother and make everything worse.

If it could get worse.

Joel had a sneaking suspicion that it would.

On the kitchen table, instead of a noon meal, were two manila envelopes: one addressed to Jared and the other to Joel.

After dumping out the contents of the envelope and skimming, Joel wasn't sure he wanted to know what Jared's said. The envelope to Joel contained a brief description of what had to be done around the house—cooking and cleaning and accounting—and a detailed description listing Ryan's, Matt's and Caleb's likes and dislikes. Billy had included a detailed calendar with the boys' schedules, from the amount of time Billy designated to help with homework to the times of their favorite television shows. He listed what they could and couldn't watch, named their bedtimes and explained their school schedule. The biggest surprise was Billy's reneging on his commitment to help with the school's upcoming Fall Festival. The notes in the margins told Joel what was expected.

He looked up slowly.

For the first time since Joel arrived, Jared wasn't frowning.

Instead, his big brother looked like he might faint.

"What does yours say?" Joel asked. For some reason, Jared's stack of papers looked a lot smaller than Joel's.

"I have a list of things to do during the evenings and the weekends with the kids." He shuffled and found a half sheet of white paper. "And this tells me what you'll be doing around the house."

The calendar in Jared's slightly shaking hand was filled in for a solid month.

Chapter Nine

Monday afternoon Beth walked down the school hallway in time to overhear her mother saying, "Mr. McCreedy, we'll find someone else to help with the festival."

The tone, condescending but logical, was one Beth knew all too well.

Help with the festival? Joel? What in the world? Beth's steps slowed to just above a crawl.

Joel didn't react quite the same way Beth usually did: obediently.

His voice sounded calm, yet firm. "Look, Mrs. Armstrong, I've a detailed list from Billy, complete with phone numbers and times. Plus, I've already met with Max this past weekend. I'm not taking over the festival. Max is willing to do that. He's filled me in on what I'm supposed to be doing and I'm just helping. I'll be taking my stepfather's place as a volunteer."

"Hi, Joel." Beth stopped, just a few feet from where Joel stood facing her mother with Caleb asleep

in his arms. Behind her, the twenty-two kindergartners following her also stopped. "You here to pick
up Matt?"

Matt stepped out of line, hurrying to the front of
it, his face contorting in fear. "Where's Grandpa?"

"We'll talk about that in the car, Matt," Joel said,
"once we get your older brother."

"Mr. McCreedy, there's already plenty of people
with experience and—" Beth's mom wasn't giving
up.

"I want Grandpa," Matt said. He wasn't giving up,
either. Beth put a hand on his shoulder.

Joel nodded to Matt. "I understand, Matt. Grandpa
will be home soon." Then, he spoke to Beth's mom.
"Sometimes the only way to get experience is to volunteer. I'm volunteering."

Beth saw her mother's expression and knew exactly what she was going to say. Unfortunately, there
was no way for Beth to intervene.

"Mr. McCreedy, given your history with another
festival at this school and what happened after—"

"If you're bringing up the missing money and in-
sinuating that I had anything to do with its disappear-
ance, I suggest you try a different tactic," Joel said
calmly. "I didn't take the money and I intend to find
out who did."

"Your brother paid the money back because he
believed you were guilty."

"Mom," Beth said firmly. "This is not the time
or place."

"My brother acted rashly. I think if you talk to him now, he'd be wanting the money back."

"The school board has some say—"

"And apparently, Billy, who completely believes in my innocence, spoke to all of them before he left," Joel said firmly. "I've even taken over the farm's accounting until Billy gets back."

Beth took a step, then another, but again stopped so quickly that one of her students bumped right into her. "Billy left?"

Mom nodded, her look of panic very much like Matt's. "On Friday, he stopped by and provided the office with all the necessary permissions when it comes to the boys, but I didn't realize how serious the situation was."

"It's not serious and it's only temporary," Joel said. "It wouldn't surprise me a bit if he cut his vacation short and came back because he knows we can't do without him."

"That's for sure." Beth's mom's words were muted but neither Beth nor Joel really needed to hear them. The expression on her face was enough.

"Mom, I need to speak to Mr. McCreedy." The words came out a bit sharper than Beth intended. Billy's absence explained a lot. It explained why Joel and his nephews had missed Sunday school yesterday and arrived late for service and then slipped out before the final prayer. It explained why Matt was wearing one of Ryan's shirts and two different colored socks. It explained why Matt's homework wasn't complete and why this morning he hadn't come to school with the Show and Share bag for his turn at show-and-tell.

"Talk some sense into him," Mom said before turning to head back to her office.

"When did Billy leave on vacation?" Beth whispered. Behind her, the kindergarten class followed as Beth practically marched Joel toward the door.

"He left Friday. I dropped the boys off at school, and when I went home for lunch there was a note from him."

"Saying what?" Beth stopped when she reached her assigned area.

"Saying," Joel replied, "that Billy was taking a much-needed vacation because he found an opportunity he didn't want to pass up."

"What kind of opportunity?"

Joel waited a moment before responding. To their left, the current principal, a megaphone in his hand, called out the names of the parents arriving and Beth's students started leaving.

Ryan's class still hadn't made it outside. Matt, with an exaggerated huff, went over and sat against a wall, far enough away from the grown-ups so they could talk without him hearing and yet close enough to them so they could tell just how annoyed he was at all he couldn't control.

"I wish we knew. Jared's called everyone he can think of."

"Why on earth would Billy pull something like this?"

To her surprise, Joel gave a lopsided grin—one that made Beth think of romantic movies, laughter and Saturday nights. "I think God's pulling something, to tell you the truth. The Sunday before Billy left, I specifically prayed that I'd start putting others first. Now, I have no choice."

"God doesn't give us any more than we can handle." Beth straightened one of her student's backpack straps and turned to face Joel again.

"I agree. God's pretty amazing. Not only have Jared and I been working together, but I've been doing some repairs this past week, started physical therapy Friday and even with all the parenting I'm doing, I haven't been laid up even once."

Parenting? Joel McCreedy parenting.

She looked at him, waiting. She'd been wondering when he'd get to the real reason he'd come home.

"I'm amazed the rumor mill hasn't already been working overtime," Joel said. "But I'm home because I'm hurt."

"How hurt?"

"Back injury, and I'm hurt enough so that doctors tell me that I'll probably need to rethink returning to bull riding. I'm going to prove them wrong."

"Why do you want to get back on the bull? You could get hurt again."

He looked a bit surprised by her comment, as if it had never occurred to him. "I'm just mad," he finally said, "that the doctors won't release me to compete now."

"Joel! Are you crazy?"

"Crazy enough to be bothered that my ten-year plan has been derailed, yes. I'm not a farmer. And although I'm more than willing to pitch in until Billy gets back, I'm not a family man. It's not what I want right now."

Not everyone had that opinion. Caleb opened one sleepy eye, took in his surroundings and nestled back under Joel's chin. Joel didn't even act like he noticed, just naturally tightened his grip and checked on Matt's behavior.

"How's Jared doing?"

The lopsided grin remained, but the look in Joel's eyes went a bit serious. He spoke in a low voice. "It's getting easier. He's stuck having to deal with me. For the boys' sake, we actually have to speak to each other. One thing I didn't realize was that he doesn't leave unless the farm needs something."

Beth nodded. When Mandy was alive, Jared had no choice but to venture out with her into Roanoke's social realm. Mandy was vivacious and loved a crowd. Jared's whole life revolved around church, home and family. As long as Mandy was part of the family, Jared *had* to venture into the world.

Without Mandy, there was no one to prod Jared,

and it seemed to most of the folks that he'd forgotten his town and church.

"Why didn't Billy make Jared get out more?" Joel wanted to know.

"I don't know," Beth admitted. "Billy was worried, but I think he attributed all of Jared's actions to grieving. He kept saying to give Jared time."

Joel nodded. "I wonder if he's thinking back to my mom. Billy always told us that he counted the days, waiting until he felt she was ready to think about dating."

"Still, with three boys, time isn't something you have much of." Beth paused, watching as two of her students made their way to a minivan where a grandfather—all smiles—waited.

One of Beth's students ran over to hug her goodbye before leaving. Almost without pause, Joel got a hug, too. Absently, he patted the little girl on the head before saying, "Billy's always been the one to go to in a pinch. I think Jared's starting to get an idea of all Billy did. I'm not the natural choice for a fill-in father. Jared's having to teach me."

"Maybe while he's teaching you, he'll decide to do it himself."

"I can only hope so. But, I'm telling you, Billy sure ran things smoothly."

Ryan's class finally exited the building. Their teacher hurried them to the spot next to Beth. The volume turned up and both Beth and Joel stood still while the safety patrol did their jobs. Ryan came to stand with Joel and Beth, dropping his backpack to the ground with a heavy thud. Matt finally left the solitude of the hard and distant brick wall, and his backpack landed next to Ryan's.

"You helping around the house?" Beth asked them.

"A whole lot," Ryan said.

Matt shook his head. "I'm not."

"You're doing fine," Joel said. "You're keeping track of what's not getting done and making sure someone hears about it."

"He tattles," Ryan translated.

"Not," Matt huffed.

"And," Joel continued, "your room is always clean."

"Because he never does anything but follow me around and mess up my room."

Joel's eyes narrowed.

Seemed for a man who said he had no parenting skills, he had more than he realized.

"Okay, time to get to the car. You two go ahead, I'll follow."

Beth walked with them across the parking lot. With Caleb nestled under his chin, Joel turned to her. "I'm pretty sure I can talk my brother into babysitting this weekend," he joked, then got serious. "I still owe you a dinner."

"You don't owe me anything," Beth responded.

"Oh, well, then good. Let's call it an old-fashioned date. I can pick you up at six Saturday evening."

More than anything, Beth wanted to say yes. But she'd heard him loud and clear. He'd said, "I'm bothered that my ten-year plan has been derailed." Then, he'd followed with, "although I'm more than willing to pitch in until Billy's gets back, I'm not a family man. It's not what I want right now."

What he'd really meant was it was not what he wanted: ever.

"I'm sorry," she murmured. "I already have plans." It wasn't a lie. She always had plans of one sort or another. Reading a book was a good plan.

"You might as well say yes now because I'm going to keep asking."

"Since you're only sticking around until the doctors release you," Beth pointed out, "I won't have to turn you down for all that long."

Joel put one hand over his heart, careful not to jostle Caleb, still held tightly under his other hand. "You wound me."

"Matt and Ryan are waiting, impatiently, and it looks like the van is locked." Matt sat on the ground, frowning, and Ryan was right beside him, busy tossing rocks across the sidewalk. Rocks that they'd now need to move back to their designated area.

For a man who wasn't a family man, Joel seemed to know what to do. While he helped Matt into the minivan and put Caleb into the car seat, Ryan cleaned up the mess he'd made. No screaming, no wasting time. Then, after Ryan climbed in, Joel drove off.

He was doing a great job.

That's when Beth realized that both Ryan's and Matt's backpacks were at her feet.

Chapter Ten

It must have been all his blustering to Beth about getting back on the circuit that made Monday seem like just one wrong move after another. When Joel got the boys home from school, he sat them in the kitchen, poured their glasses of milk and told them to do homework.

That's what Billy did.

When he went back a little while later to check on them, the milk glasses were empty and still on the table, but the boys were gone. Joel found them in the backyard. Caleb had woken up and was chasing Ryan. Ryan had a ball and was zipping around the yard. It seemed the object of his game was to throw the ball at Matt, who was pouting and sitting under a tree. About the time Joel opened his mouth to put a stop to the harassment, Ryan managed to hit Matt in the face with the ball and his nose started to bleed.

Caleb found the blood fascinating.

Matt wailed.

Ryan couldn't quite hide a smile. Of course, he stopped smiling when Joel sent him to his room. After getting Matt cleaned up, Joel put Matt and Caleb in front of the television. Because of his hurt nose, Joel let Matt pick the program. Caleb wasn't happy with the choice and started droning, "Wanna watch trains. Wanna watch trains. Wanna watch…"

Things went from bad to worse, making Joel wish he were out in the field with Jared.

Joel left the hamburger buns in the oven too long and they burnt. Plus, no one had gone grocery shopping over the weekend and they were out of onions, ketchup and pickles. Ryan, still smarting from an hour in his room, was the only one not to make a big deal out of having to eat either a plain burger or a burger with only mustard.

After dinner, Jared went to give Caleb his bath while Joel put away the dishes before helping with homework. That's when he discovered *why* the boys hadn't done their homework earlier.

Their backpacks were at school.

Heading up the stairs and to the kids' bathroom, he poked his head in and asked Jared, "What do you do when the kids leave their backpacks at school?"

Jared almost laughed. "Both of them?"

"Both of them," Joel responded.

"How did that happen?"

"Well, I was talking to Beth—"

"I yike Beth." Caleb chose that moment to splash. To Joel's surprise, Jared didn't even blink, just splashed back and said, "I think your uncle likes her, too."

"So, do we skip homework?" Joel asked.

Jared thought for a moment. "I'm trying to remember what Mandy did."

Since Joel's return, a week and a half ago—had it really been such a short time?—Jared hadn't mentioned Mandy's name even once.

Joel waited a moment, just to gauge Jared's mood, and then asked, "What would Billy do?"

"Call their teachers."

Well, duh. Joel knew who Matt's teacher was but not Ryan's. "Who's teaching second grade now?"

Caleb splashed again. This time Jared didn't respond. After a moment, Joel's brother shook his head. "I don't know. Mrs. Kelly retired last year." In wonderment, he said, "I don't know who my son's teacher is."

"All I need to do," Joel offered, "is ask Ryan. He'll know his teacher's name. Then, when I call Beth, she can give me the phone number."

"I yike Beth," Caleb repeated. This time, the splash was of tsunami proportions. Jared's hair got wet and so did the front of Joel's shirt. Caleb laughed.

After a moment, so did Joel, but not his brother. Jared retreated back under the chip on his shoulder, where all was safe and he didn't have to worry about who was teaching his son's second grade class.

It was on the tip of Joel's tongue to tell his brother that everything and everyone would be okay, especially Ryan. Instead, the doorbell rang and from downstairs came a shout, "I'll get it."

"We're not expecting anyone, and Billy wouldn't ring the doorbell," Jared said. "You'd better go check."

By the time Joel made it down the stairs, Ryan was ushering Beth in and Matt was sitting on the chair, legs stuck out in front of him, staring at the television as if he were a wooden puppet.

"Glad it's not my teacher," Ryan teased.

She dangled two backpacks in one hand. "Forget something?"

Ryan moaned. "Now we have to do homework."

Joel turned off the television and simply nodded.

The boys didn't get anything to drink, not so close to bedtime, especially not Matt. This time, Beth made sure the pencils were sharpened; she even knew where the sharpener was. While the boys started their work—Ryan doing double-digit addition and Matt finding and circling every letter *G* in a story—Beth went through their backpacks.

"Matt should have the Show and Share bag here somewhere," she said. "Today was his turn at show-and-tell."

"You missed show-and-tell?"

If Joel were to believe Ryan's tone, missing show-and-tell was pretty serious stuff.

"I can't find the bag," Matt admitted. "I had it in my room all weekend and this morning it was gone."

"But you're the one who always has a clean room," Joel remembered.

"Caleb likes going in there and taking his stuff," Ryan said. "He used to like taking my stuff, too, but he's scared of me."

Matt's eyes started to fill, again.

"I'll go look for it," Joel offered.

"Don't cry," Beth soothed Matt. "Do your *G* paper, and I'll go with Joel. After all, I know exactly what it looks like."

Joel had been in Matt's room a time or two. He even knew, thanks to Ryan, that Beth was the one who'd painted the murals in each of the boys' rooms. Matt's mural was of Winnie the Pooh. The room was ridiculously clean for a boy of five. Beth saved him from having to bend down and look under the bed. She did it. While she was on the floor, her cell phone beeped. She pulled it from her shirt pocket, checked it and ignored it. Next, she opened the closet and then looked behind the door. No Show and Share bag.

They moved on to Caleb's room. It looked like someone had turned it upside down, and then just for fun, turned it upside down again. The toys from his birthday party, just over a week ago, were strewn across the room. Half-formed wooden train tracks made walking difficult. Fittingly, his mural was a train.

"I guess that's next on my list," Joel said. "Trying to keep their rooms clean."

"No," Beth said gently. "You need to teach them to keep their rooms clean."

"Caleb's a little young."

"He's the perfect age to start." She bent, moved a rocking horse to the side and picked up a giant teddy bear. Around its neck was a blue jean bag. In glittering letters, the bag read Show and Share. She dumped about a dozen trains from the bag and handed it to Joel. "Fill this tomorrow and send it to school with him."

"Fill it with what?"

"Matt gets to decide."

"That's not fun," Joel said. "I think I'd like to decide."

"Decide what Matt shares with the class?"

"Sure," Joel said. "First, I'd make the bag a bit bigger."

"Why?"

Maybe it was because he was already acting out of character, taking on a pseudo Mr. Mom persona. Maybe it was because tonight had started out so very wrong, and now standing close to Beth in Caleb's tiny bedroom felt so right. He could smell her perfume and wanted to reach out and tuck an errant strand of hair behind her ear just so he could touch her.

Or maybe it was because she was just so cute and also so innocent. She had no idea the turmoil she was causing. Every time he turned around, she was there. Half the time acting like he was a pest, and the other half of the time looking at him with those doe eyes that could bring him to his knees and make him start rethinking his ten-year plan.

"Why?" he repeated slowly. "Because, if it were up to me, I'd put myself in that bag and let Matt convince you that I'm a prized possession."

If it hadn't been for Jared entering Caleb's room, carrying a towel-clad little boy and shooing them out, Beth wasn't sure how long they'd have stayed.

Who knew Joel McCreedy had the heart of a poet?

Ryan, old enough to be responsible for himself, was finishing his homework. Matt, already finished, was now taking his turn in the bath.

Beth was very aware of Joel walking down the stairs beside her, so close he could easily take her hand. He opened the front door and escorted her outside.

Truly, she meant to get in her car, head home and watch some television. Instead, when he motioned toward the porch swing, she sat.

With him right next to her.

In the books she read, the women always came up with snappy dialogue, intimate jokes or something fantastic to talk about. Her favorite topics with her friends were church, books and work. Not exactly guy topics. With her sisters the conversation flowed, mostly on their end, but Beth could hold her own. They didn't favor work or books, but church was always a good topic. Right now, her middle sister only wanted to talk about when the baby came. Her oldest sister favored news of any new single guys in town. Again, not guy topics.

Unfortunately, she had a hard enough time talking with a man she wasn't attracted to. She'd never *ever* been at ease in the company of someone she found appealing. Now she couldn't think of a word to say except the tried-and-true and the boring. "Looks like Matt tried really hard on his homework."

Joel surprised her. "I agree he did it very neatly, but he grips the pencil so tightly I'm half-afraid it's going to break. Plus, he circled just as many *C*s as *G*s. Is that typical? When looking for *G*s, are the other kids circling *C*s, as well?"

"That's one of the things I want to talk to Jared about."

Did she imagine it or did Joel stretch and manage to edge just a tiny bit closer to her? The porch swing didn't allow for much wiggle room and Joel's proximity, at the moment, really didn't allow for any wiggle at all.

Beth felt every nerve ending wake up and take notice. She thought about standing, but she didn't want to.

She liked it right where she was.

As if reading her mind, Joel commented, "Well, I'm not giving up the best seat in the house to my brother. I did that all the while I was growing up. Tonight, the porch swing's mine. And yours." He used his toe to push off the porch and gently started the swing moving.

"You know," he added, "the swing really is mine. I made one in shop class. It's on the back porch. Then, because I knew I could do it better on my own, I made this one."

She relaxed, taking in the night air, which was heavy with the scent of the upcoming winter weather—and the scent of him.

"I could make you one," he offered.

"So," she began, more from nervousness than a need to talk, "if you have time to make me a porch swing, you plan on sticking around for a while."

"At least six months."

"You said you came back because you were hurt. Surely you had a home somewhere. Why did you decide to come here?"

The swinging slowed. Joel leaned back, looking at the stars. "Honestly," he said, more to the stars than to her, "I haven't felt like I've had a home since I left. In the back of my mind, I guess, I still considered this home and thought I'd come back. Of course, I always pictured the homecoming with a bit more fanfare." He laughed, but it was a low mirthful sound that spoke of dreams both lost and fulfilled.

"The night I came home," he continued, "for a brief moment when my truck idled at the front gate, I almost believed in second chances."

"Fresh start." Beth understood the concept, and in some ways longed to experience it herself. Not that she'd know how. Her whole world was here, but she sometimes felt suffocated, sometimes felt like she was in a rut. Her cell phone beeped. With a sigh, she pulled it from her pocket, noted her mother's name on the caller ID and turned the thing completely off. She didn't need to answer it now and have to explain to her mother where she was or what she was doing.

"Except, my fresh start hasn't gotten off to much of a start." Joel closed his eyes and leaned back. He might be sitting next to her on the porch swing, he might be offering himself as a prize and asking her out to dinner, but one thing was for sure, this man was not relaxed.

No matter how he pretended.

The crickets got louder as the night shadows grew. Since Joel's return, Beth's bedtime had gotten later and later. Her dreams left her discontented and feeling like there was something out there, just ready for her to grab, but she could never quite get a grip or even know exactly what it was she was reaching for.

At the moment, though, she wasn't tired, not with Joel sitting next to her and an Iowa cornfield spread around her.

"What happened that night?" she said softly. "Why did you leave if you were so tired, so tired that you drove off the road?"

"The best thing that happened that night was seeing Billy. Watching him run down the porch steps and give me a welcoming hug. I'd been on the road all day and, boy, was I stiff. I thought for a moment he'd knock me over."

"He didn't know you were hurting?"

"I needed the welcome far more than I needed to avoid pain," Joel remembered.

"What else did Billy do?"

"He told me that they'd missed me and that I'd lost weight. He promised to put some weight back on me."

"Sounds like Billy."

Joel didn't respond. His toe still slowly, very slowly, edged the swing back and forth. His arm was still pressed against hers, but he was somewhere else, somewhere in the stars he seemed so fascinated by.

Beth was torn. She needed to leave. With every word, he was inviting her into his private torments, using her as a friend and confidante, telling her that she mattered and was needed—wanted. Being needed was nothing new. Her students needed her and thanked her with hugs and smiles. Her sisters needed her. She was always available to run an errand, like fetching bubblegum ice cream, or taking in a last-minute movie on a Friday night if the latest Mr. Right suddenly became Mr. Canceled-at-the-Last-Minute. Her mother needed her, all too often—needed her to be the one daughter who did everything right.

Feeling wanted? Now, that was a role she wasn't exactly comfortable with.

But she couldn't leave. The warmth of his body and the weight of his words held her prisoner.

"What did Jared do?" Beth finally asked, when it looked like Joel wasn't going to continue talking.

"I managed to regain my footing and asked him if I was invited in."

"And Jared invited you?"

"Nope, he didn't say a word. Just stood in front of the door. Billy did, though, he invited me. He even said they had ham left over from dinner and that it was too bad my nephews were asleep. I'd have to wait until the morning to see them."

"What time was it?"

"Almost nine."

Beth thought back. Yes, that was just after she'd been there, wanting to take on Jared for missing his parent-teacher conference. If Jared had been willing to listen, to talk, she'd have been at the farm when Joel arrived. Instead, Jared had claimed bad timing, and in just five minutes Beth's home visit was over.

She'd headed to the McClanahans' to drop off something for her mother, and so she'd witnessed Joel driving off the road. What she'd thought would be a one-time good deed had turned into sitting on the porch swing with the one man she didn't dare fall in love with. Definitely falling in love.

Joel probably had no idea what her thoughts were. And she needed to change their direction before she did something stupid like grab Joel, hug him, tell him that she'd like to be the one to fix dinner and put some weight on him, *forever*.

Um, maybe Joel did have an idea. His eyes opened and he changed the way he was sitting. He no longer leaned back, but did more of a slouch, toward her. His long legs stretched forward, his cowboy boots heel down on the hard planks of the porch. Nonchalantly, he placed his arm around the back of the porch swing, just barely touching her shoulders. Upstairs, from an open window, they could hear the sound of Matt talking to his father. Jared's deep voice sounded and Beth could just make out his words.

"I'll listen to you say your prayers."

Joel must have been listening to Jared, too, because he said, "I did pray, but I had nowhere to go, no money, and if you'd have asked me when I pulled up in front of Solitaire Farm if I had pride, I'd have said, 'No, none left.'"

"I think quite a few prayers were answered that night, and pride can be overrated. Doesn't the Bible say that pride breeds quarrels?"

"I wasn't looking for a quarrel that night. I was looking for a bed." Joel's voice deepened. "And, believe me, my pride reared up at the sight of my brother standing on the porch, blocking the entryway and not inviting me in."

"So you left, as tired as you were."

What Joel said next fairly rang with pride. "I took off my cowboy hat, slapped it against my thigh and said I didn't need a meal or an invite to come in. I was just in the neighborhood and wanted to say hi."

"What did Jared say?"

"He said 'good.'"

Beth couldn't even imagine her sisters acting like Joel and his brother. All Beth had to do was pick up the phone, and they'd come running and vice versa.

Her mother, too, would walk on hot coals to make sure her daughters had everything they needed.

"He didn't mean it."

Joel's fingers drifted from the back of the porch swing and gently brushed against her shoulder. He wasn't looking at the stars now. He was looking at her. "Oh, yes, he did."

Then, Joel McCreedy said exactly what she expected him to say and she reminded herself why he was the man she shouldn't fall in love with. He focused on her and said, "But that's okay. Real cowboys get back in the saddle, doesn't matter if they have broken bones, concussions or slipped disks. I want nothing more than to get back in the saddle. I just need six months to heal."

Beth felt her throat tighten. His words shouldn't be a surprise, and she had no right to feel hurt. A cowboy was always thinking of his next ride, didn't matter how hurt he was.

Or, who he hurt.

She stood, right when his fingers stopped gently dancing on her shoulder, right before his touch turned into a caress and she lost the ability to think. "Six months isn't that long," she said.

"It's feeling like forever," he said, sitting up and scooting over so she'd have more room when she sat down again.

Obviously it didn't occur to Joel that she wouldn't sit back down.

For the first time, Beth considered that the only

person Joel *really* had was his brother, Jared. And, even knowing that, and knowing that Jared was in a bind right now, Joel was already thinking about when he'd get to leave.

Which is why Beth should never place her heart in Joel's care. He much too easily turned his back on those who loved him.

So Beth turned her back to him. No way did she want him to see that he'd hurt her. Then, as she walked across the porch and down the front steps, she said the words that usually came from his lips.

"It's time for me to go."

Chapter Eleven

Joel watched Beth's taillights until they disappeared down the driveway, turning in the direction of the McClanahan place. His time on the porch with Beth was the highlight of a long day. Until she left, that is, and Joel wasn't sure whether it was his timing or his company that sent her running home.

Finding out would give him something to look forward to.

The moment he stepped inside the house, he wanted to go back outside. From upstairs came the sound of loud, continuous wailing.

"Ryan, are you still doing your homework?" he yelled.

"I don't whine like a girl," Ryan protested, from the kitchen.

Taking the steps two at a time, Joel headed up the stairs and skidded to a stop at the top. Jared leaned against Matt's door.

"What happened?" Joel asked.

"I listened to his prayer, I said good-night and then I went to turn on his action hero night-light."

"So?"

"It won't work."

"All those screams are because his night-light won't work?"

Jared nodded, looking shell-shocked. "Is Beth still here? Think she'd know what to do? She's his teacher."

"And you're his father."

For a moment, Joel thought his brother would shut down. Instead, Jared turned around and went back into his son's bedroom. Instead of yelling, Joel heard Jared talking, asking about monsters and explaining that he'd already walked the house and there were no monsters. After just a moment, Jared marched from the room, went into his own bedroom and then came out with a big flashlight.

In an instant, Joel knew exactly why Billy took off, and it wasn't just so the brothers would be forced to get along. It would be so Jared would be forced to remember fatherhood.

It was Jared remembering how to be a brother that had Joel worried.

Because Joel wasn't sure he remembered how to be a brother, either.

Heading back down the stairs, Joel checked on Ryan in the kitchen. Two more math problems and the kid was done. Joel opened the freezer, grabbed two Popsicle treats, threw one to Ryan and headed back into the living room to sit in front of the television.

Switching through the channels, he tried to find something, anything, that interested him. But television didn't have a chance. Joel's life had more drama, more action and more situation comedy than any show on prime time.

Upstairs, the wailing finally stopped, tapering off to a few sobs. After a moment, Jared came back downstairs. First he checked the kitchen, told Ryan to "get a move on" and then came and sat down in the easy chair that Billy usually claimed.

"I take it you calmed Matt down."

"He's sleeping with my flashlight. He thinks it's pretty cool."

"Looks like you're going to need a new flashlight."

Jared chuckled. "Small price to pay." He hopped up, went in and got his own Popsicle, and came back to stare at the television.

In some ways, it was the brothers' first time alone—alone without some sort of major conflict to deal with, not like the first night Joel had arrived home.

"Jared, you tell your brother he's welcome here," Billy had ordered.

"I don't have to," Jared had stated.

And Joel had responded with, "I don't want to cause any problems. I'll go."

Maybe it was the talk outside with Beth that had brought everything to the surface again. Joel couldn't seem to shake the sense of loss he felt, concerning both his career and his family ties.

Eight years ago, Joel had willingly left. Not quite two weeks ago, he'd almost done it again, almost turned his back on Solitaire Farm. He'd climbed behind the wheel, started the engine and drove back down the winding driveway. In the rearview mirror, the farm had gotten smaller and smaller until it disappeared.

He'd come that close to driving away forever.

"When will your truck be repaired?" Jared finally asked.

"Why, you thinking I need something to drive away in?"

Jared didn't chuckle, instead looked grim like always. "No, that's not why I'm asking. Truth is, with you here, I kinda miss seeing that wreck parked out by the barn."

Joel recognized a safe subject when he heard one. "Tiny says he's located a couple replacement doors. Now he's just trying to negotiate the best price."

"You could probably buy a new one and save money."

"I agree. Keeping up a fifty-year-old truck takes time and dedication, but she's got an engine I can work on myself, and she's got a body that can plow into a fence and still keep her shape. There's a lot to be said for old-fashioned."

"She looks a lot like she did back when you finished working on her."

Joel agreed. "I've taken good care of her. No need for much change. Not like around here. You've done quite a bit."

"I haven't changed the place that much," Jared protested.

"Not the inside, although the place feels smaller. The outside looks changed, quite a bit. I'm amazed that you put in a farm stand just a half mile from the front gate."

When Jared didn't answer, Joel went back to something safe. "I half expected Rambo to come running out, barking at me like I'd never left."

"Place is the same size, I promise you. Rambo died when Ryan was a year old. We talked about getting another dog, but then Mandy got pregnant with Matt and we had enough on our plates."

"Rambo was a working dog," Joel said. "He'd be hard to replace."

"Yes, Rambo worked hard clear up until he turned fourteen. Then, he was a geriatric dog and Mandy took care of him right alongside Ryan."

"You remember how Rambo used to whine the few times Mom didn't let him tag along when she made a trip into town?"

"I remember," Jared said.

"Mom would have liked Solitaire's Market," Joel remarked. "She'd have worked it."

"Yeah, and we sure could have used her help. We needed the money once Mandy took sick. I got online and started researching small farms that were making additional money and how they were doing it. In the big city, Walgreens is the yuppie one-stop shop. In the country, a farmer's market is the draw. It's been extra work, but it's what kept us going."

"I've got to pick up my truck this coming week. I'm afraid to ask how much I owe Tiny. Then, there are the medical bills, which are sure enough breaking me," Joel admitted. "I received three in the mail today. Of course, one was for a whopping forty-three cents. The other two were in the hundreds."

Jared finished his Popsicle and stood. "Well," he said in a quiet voice that Joel recognized as disapproval, "you'll live. When you leave this time, though, just remember we've got no money left to give you or for you to take."

Before Joel could respond, Jared was up the stairs. The only proof that he'd actually sat in the same living room as Joel and carried on a conversation was a crumpled white Popsicle wrapper.

Joel had the uneasy feeling he'd missed an opportunity to extend an olive branch.

Yes, some things had changed; others weren't about to, not yet, like Joel's ability to ask for forgiveness and Jared's ability to forgive.

* * *

"Well," said Linda on Tuesday evening, when Beth got home, "I thought you'd never get here. Are you going to tell me why it took you so long last night to drop off two backpacks?"

"I wasn't gone that long."

The two sisters shared the small house that had once belonged to their grandmother. Until Beth's college graduation, Mom had rented it out, using what extra she got from rent to help with Beth's college tuition.

Linda sat at the kitchen table, having just finished putting on bright red nail polish. She held her hands in the air, wiggling them so they'd dry.

"You have a date tonight?" Beth asked.

"No, but I'm hoping you do."

Beth set her books on the table, grabbed a soda from the fridge and sat across from Linda. Without prompting, Linda took Beth's hand and started removing the old polish.

"I don't, but it's not because Joel hasn't asked. Every time he gets me alone, he asks."

Linda leaned forward. "And how did he get you alone last night?"

"Porch swing, after we'd found the lost Show and Share bag in Caleb's bedroom."

"Find anything else in little Caleb's room?"

"Nope, just found my way down the stairs and out the front door. Then Joel suggested we sit on the porch swing."

"I can't remember the last time I sat on a porch swing with someone that good-looking," Linda mourned.

"Go over to Solitaire Farm. Joel just might suggest it."

Linda finished Beth's right hand and started on the left. "Not a chance. Ever since that cowboy rode back into town, the only thing he's aimed his lasso at is you."

"Unfortunately," Beth said, "his lasso is short-term. And then there's Mom."

Linda probably didn't know how perfect an analogy she'd started. Beth knew. She found the info in one of the many books she'd devoured. A hundred years ago, when cowboys had to ride over acres of land to find and brand the calves, they'd often had to deal with distressed mother cows.

Linda rolled her eyes. "You can't let Mom rule your life." Holding up a perfectly manicured hand, she added, "I know Mom means well. But, since Dad died, her ideas and dreams are a bit skewed."

Truth was, Beth didn't even recall her father. She knew he'd been a truck driver, which didn't seem to match her mother's personality. He'd also, according to Susan and Linda, been pretty rough-and-tumble, some more traits that didn't seem to complement Mom.

Beth wondered what her mom had been like before Allen Armstrong died.

"This time, though," Beth said, "Mom has some

reasons. There's the missing money, the fact that Joel never came back when Jared needed him, and even now, with his back injury, the only thing Joel wants is to ride a bull."

Linda finished another nail and reached over to take a drink from her little sister's soda. "Do you really think Joel took the money?"

"When it first happened, absolutely not. Of course, I was all of fourteen and…"

"And in love with Joel even back then."

Beth blushed. "It was just a teenage crush."

"What are you calling it now?"

Beth didn't hesitate. She'd lost plenty of sleep thinking about what to call it now. "An impractical infatuation."

Linda snorted, finished Beth's last nail and said, "Take off your shoes and I'll do your feet."

Beth hesitated, then said, "Use that pretty green shade."

"Green? You've always been a plain pink kind of girl. Hmm." Linda obeyed and refrained from making a snide comment. That Beth didn't need or want wild colors had always fascinated Linda, who considered herself a bit Bohemian.

"If I let you practice on me, I get some say," Beth reminded her.

"So, let's go back to my original question." Linda opened the green nail polish. "Do you really think, right now, today, that Joel took the money?"

Beth thought back to what Joel had said yesterday

to her mother, concerning slander. She thought about him having enough pride to drive away from Solitaire Farm so tired even that he'd fallen asleep at the wheel. She thought about his indignation at the Ice Cream Shack when Billy had brought up the theft.

He'd acted surprised, but even more, he'd acted offended.

But surely during his few phone calls home, Joel had been questioned by Billy. Thanks to Mandy, Beth knew that Billy took Joel's calls. Jared didn't.

Could the rift between the two brothers have ended if Jared had given in a little? Talked to Joel? Said what was on his mind?

Would Joel have come home sooner?

Joel, at least, was making up for lost time now, though, helping with homework and carpool duties, burning hot dogs, if the smell in last night's kitchen was any indication, and pitching in at the very festival he was accused of stealing from.

"He didn't take the money." Saying the words was very liberating. Beth felt like a burden had been lifted. She started to get up, but Linda still held her foot and was only on the middle toe.

Linda pulled Beth's foot a bit closer. "Stay still," she ordered. "And as for wanting to get back to the rodeo, can you think of any cowboy who doesn't want that, especially one who's done as well as Joel?"

Beth knew exactly how well Joel had done. He'd been on television a dozen times, and he'd made the local paper, too. Plus, Linda, who followed the show, especially a few years ago when she'd been dating a bull rider, had not only kept track of Joel's career but often informed Beth of what was going on.

"Did you know he'd been hurt?" Beth asked.

"No, and I'm surprised to hear it. The last rodeo he participated in was Lovington, and he was in the top three. He didn't lose his seat, did his eight seconds and he landed on his feet."

"He says he didn't know he'd hurt himself," Beth said. "He said he woke up the next morning and it was hard to walk. In a matter of hours, he couldn't walk. Pretty soon, he knew he needed to come home."

"I remember thinking he'd been extremely lucky that day," Linda admitted.

"Why?"

"He'd drawn a good bull, one with plenty of attitude, who'd help him win. Homeless had tossed two bull riders the week before."

"Homeless was the bull's name?"

"Meaning he didn't allow a rider to make himself comfortable on his back." Linda finished Beth's last toe.

"Pretty spot-on name considering he made Joel homeless."

Linda nodded, seeming lost in thought. "Maybe that bull and that tumble were exactly what Joel needed." When Beth didn't answer, Linda stood and began to gather up her nail supplies. "You up for a movie?"

"I'm pretty tired."

"Yeah, you've been losing lots of sleep."

"I wasn't out that late!"

"You were out late enough that Mom called three times."

"You've waited until now to tell me that?" Beth said, taken aback.

"I was asleep when you came home last night. You were gone went I woke up this morning."

"You could have written a note."

"I didn't want to ruin your day."

"A call from Mom doesn't ruin my day."

"If that were true, you would have answered your cell phone when she called last night."

"How did you know…?"

"You might want to listen to the answering machine. Mom got pretty annoyed the third time she called. I answered the first time, and then I started screening the calls. Unfortunately, Brad Pitt didn't call even once, and Mom really didn't want to talk to me."

"Another reason why I need to keep turning Joel down when he asks me out. I may believe he didn't steal the money. What he's doing now with Jared's family may do wonders to erase the years of absence. But Mom totally dislikes him."

Linda nodded. "Mom's disliked every single guy I've dated. You were away at college, so you don't know how much grief Susan went through the year she was dating Alex. Here's the truth, Beth, and you better think about it. The kind of guy Mom wants for us doesn't exist."

Beth opened her mouth in an attempt to respond, but Linda wasn't finished. "He doesn't exist, and if we look for him, we'll be like her. Still alone twenty years from now."

Chapter Twelve

Joel quickly learned to time his arrival at church so that he didn't have to go into the ten-minute meet and greet. In a grand swoop through the vestibule and down the stairs, he deposited each kid in the appropriate classroom, saving Matt for last, of course.

Opening the door, he peeked in and spotted Beth standing in the front of the room. He winked—that seemed to be their greeting of choice—and suggested, "Dinner, this evening?"

Maybe he imagined it, but her "no" sounded halfhearted rather than firm. Unfortunately, with a classroom of a dozen five-and six-year-old witnesses, now was not the time to ratchet up the old McCreedy charm. Just wait until after church.

He hurried to get his favorite back pew. Most heads didn't turn, nope, some of the members were getting used to seeing him. Some were even starting to accept him. Many of them had realized that the only way they'd hear any updates about Billy would be if they befriended, or at least pretended to befriend, Joel.

This morning Nathan Fisher and his youth group were presenting the lesson. Joel had learned to respect the man. As a physical therapist, he was top-notch. He seemed to devote as much time and energy to being a youth minister. Joel shifted in his seat. A decade ago, he'd been sitting with the teenagers, taking part and helping with services. Fisher hadn't been a youth director back then. He'd probably been a snot-nosed kid sitting with the youth group of some other church, waiting to grow up and not make the same kind of mistakes as Joel.

Mistakes like not doing things for his family and not doing things for the Lord.

Joel tried not to think about Fisher as the competition for Beth's affection. They'd gone out, Joel knew, but not often, which told Joel that they were more friends than anything else.

Jared had married his best friend. Come to think of it, so had Max and Derek.

Opening the bulletin, Joel tried not to hear the lesson the youth group was presenting. It was near impossible because teenagers had one volume, same as second-graders and three-year-olds: loud.

The lesson had to do with the apostle Paul and how he was a hero. Yet, the reasons the youth group presented had to do with Paul's refusal to take money from the people of Corinth. Especially notable was that the people of Corinth didn't respect him, not as much as they respected the super apostles.

Joel hadn't even heard the term *super apostles*. He'd have to ask Fisher at therapy in the morning.

Another reason Paul was a hero had to do with how he carried his guilt and how humble he was. He was nothing, he claimed, the least of the apostles.

Then, the teens acted out all the punishments Paul had lived, from floggings to shipwrecks to imprisonment.

Still, Paul continued to serve.

In the last eight years, Joel hadn't stepped up to help with communion or even drive someone to church. All his floggings, shipwrecks and imprisonments were the direct results of either the bull or poor choices—his own. About the only good deed he'd done lately, when it came to serving the Lord, was driving the boys to church.

It was a place to start.

Finally, the teenagers sat down and Fisher went back to the podium. Joel turned his attention to the bulletin. After skimming the song selection and the tithes collected last week, he went to the announcements. There was a ladies' class on Thursday morning. The pantry needed both dry spaghetti and peanut butter. And, in two weeks, there was a baby shower planned for Susan Farraday. With a start, Joel realized that the shower was for Beth's sister. An idea formed. He'd have to carve out time even as he carved out the pieces. He'd make Susan a cradle, a little wooden cradle, and he'd engrave the baby's name on it. And after he gave the thing to Susan, he'd turn to Beth and ask her out for dinner again.

Maybe then her halfhearted *no* would turn into a full-hearted yes. And if it stayed a no, he'd at least have Susan on his side.

A loud amen from Fisher brought Joel back to the sermon at hand. Joel should have felt guilty for letting his thoughts wander. Instead, he reached forward and for the first time in years took hold of the Bible.

It felt good; it felt right.

Two weeks later, Joel had finished making the cradle for Susan in time to drop it off at her shower.

The following Monday morning, Joel parked the minivan in the school lot and escorted the boys inside and to the playground. This time Beth wasn't on duty. Ryan, figuring out the boy-girl thing way too early, swaggered down the hallway. "Uncle Joel likes a *girlll.*"

Joel didn't mind. "Someday you will, too."

"Nope," Ryan responded, dead serious. "I'm going to be a bull rider."

Joel could only hope Ryan never said that near his father.

Matt walked slower. His uncle wanted to speak with his teacher, and even though he knew he wasn't in trouble, that just wasn't the stuff a kindergartner's dreams were made of.

As for Caleb, he didn't care. He'd figured out last

week that every time Joel went into Miss Beth's room, Caleb got a sticker. The world was good.

"Morning," Joel greeted Beth, stepping into the room and quickly heading for the cubbies to drop off Matt's lunch box. Matt was perfectly capable of depositing his lunch box where it needed to go, but Joel needed a reason to stop by every morning.

"Morning, Joel."

"You free for dinner tonight?"

"It will be too late after our Fall Festival meeting."

"Gotta eat something," Joel responded.

"I yike to eat," Caleb added helpfully.

"I'll probably go home and make something before the meeting. There will be time."

"Where are you living now?" Joel knew perfectly well she lived in her grandmother's old house. Jared gave up that information. Joel also knew that Beth lived with her oldest sister, Linda, and that Linda wasn't living up to Mrs. Armstrong's strict standards. Joel could only hope that Linda had some influence on Beth.

"I'm living on Oak, in my grandmother's house."

"I always liked your grandmother."

"And she liked you."

It was true. Anne Armstrong had been Beth's grandmother on her father's side. Joel couldn't remember Mr. Armstrong, but he knew from Billy that Beth's dad had died in a rock climbing accident when Beth was just a few years old.

"You need any work done around the house? I'm pretty handy."

"How's your back?"

"I'm heading to the physical therapist after I leave here. I'm hoping to scale down from three visits a week to two."

Did he imagine it or had a shadow flashed across her face? A slight droop of her lips, those very kissable lips, followed by their tightening, which meant he'd said something wrong. "I'm feeling much better. And I'm hungry all the time. It sure gets lonely eating alone."

"With your brother and three boys to take care of, I doubt you're ever alone. I'm not available tonight and I need to get some things prepped for class. Thanks for bringing Matt's stuff by."

And just like that, he was dismissed.

He'd never understand females. Even if she didn't want to have dinner with him, she should be glad he was feeling better and trying to limit how many times he saw the physical therapist.

And, he realized not even a minute later, she should be glad he happened to be in the room. He recognized the little girl being helped into the room while hysterically sobbing into the side of an older student. It was Mitzi Gabor. Her mother, Mona, had been at Caleb's birthday party. She'd asked a lot of pointed questions, enough so that when Joel saw her at church, he headed the other way.

Mitzi was crying hard, and she held a hand over her mouth.

Beth moved from behind her desk. "Mitzi, are you all right?"

Mitzi sobbed even louder. At first, Joel thought the hand over her mouth was preventing her from answering, but then she moved her hand, and he could see the blood. Joel looked at Beth. She'd stopped moving.

"Beth, what's wrong?"

Even the older student seemed frozen, looking from Mitzi to Mitzi's teacher.

Pale didn't begin to describe the color Beth's face was turning. Okay, Joel'd seen this a time or two before, with rookie bull riders who suddenly realized that their career was probably over because they couldn't stand the sight of blood.

"Sit down," Joel ordered Beth. When she didn't, he went to his knees in front of Mitzi and gently turned her so she faced him and not Beth.

"What happened?"

Mitzi couldn't answer, so the older student did. "She walked too close to someone swinging on the swings and got kicked in the mouth."

To prove it, Mitzi opened her mouth. Joel was glad Beth couldn't see. She'd have passed out. One tooth tilted at an angle, assuring Joel that it wasn't long for Mitzi's mouth. There was so much blood in her mouth that he couldn't see anything except for the two top teeth and the seriously compromised bottom one.

"Did you bite your tongue?"

She shook her head.

"Why didn't you take her to the nurse?" Joel asked.

"We don't have a school nurse except once a week."

Joel should have known that. From the time Billy married Joel's mother, many a meal conversation had focused on the dreaded phrase *budget cuts*.

Right now, Joel had a different kind of cut to deal with, but first he had to find it. Leading Mitzi to the bathroom in Beth's classroom, he motioned for the older student to hold open the door while he ushered Mitzi inside. A quick glance in Beth's direction showed him that she was getting some color back.

He encouraged Mitzi to spit blood into the sink and took a few paper towels to help clean up the little girl. A minute later, her mouth was rinsed, and a tooth was clutched in her fist.

"I'll get shome money," Mitzi said. "The toof fairy will come tonight." Her face was still moist with tears, but her eyes were shining.

Joel looked back at Beth. She was already heading his way. "Do we need to send her home?" he asked.

She crouched down and Mitzi willingly went into her arms. A few murmured words, a few strokes to the head and one tiny tooth carefully put into a special envelope made for a happily-ever-after.

Mitzi even went back outside for the last five minutes of before-school play. Her only problem now was that Beth wouldn't let her take the tooth with her.

"That's why I didn't recognize you the first day," Joel said.

"What?"

"That's why I didn't recognize you the first day. You barely looked me full in the face. I was bleeding. You can't stand the sight of blood. All I ever really got was a side view. I feel much better now. I've been kicking myself. Now, you owe me dinner."

When she didn't answer, he let it be. She was still pale enough for him to cut her some slack.

Ten minutes later he entered Fisher's therapy center and signed in. Sometimes Joel was the only one in the place. Other times, like today, there'd be one or two other people. A large brunette rode the stationary bike. Joel didn't know her. The other occupant was Frank Peabody, who was married to the nurse who'd admitted Joel to the hospital just over four weeks ago. He'd been a mailman for almost fifty years and was recovering from a broken hip.

"I like coming here," Frank said. "It gets me out of the house."

"He comes for the massages," Fisher threw in.

Joel completely understood. He'd be willing to come here forever if it meant being wrapped in the hot packs, followed by a massage.

"What's new today?" Frank asked. "You finally convince Beth to go out with you?"

"I'm getting closer."

Fisher, who shouldn't be giving advice since he had his eye on Beth, too, said, "Maybe you should try something new. Instead of asking her out, send her flowers or something."

"Did that work for you?"

"True," Fisher agreed. "Maybe I need to follow my own advice. Girls like things like flowers and cards."

"Joel would never send a card," Frank said. "The entire eight years he was gone, not one letter, not even a postcard."

"Maybe I emailed," Joel protested.

Frank raised an eyebrow. He knew better. "Some people said you stayed away because of guilt."

Finally, somebody had the guts to come out and say what they were really thinking. But while Joel had been waiting for just such a moment, now that it was here, he felt somewhat ill prepared. Maybe because just being accused made him *feel* guilty.

"Maybe those people should ask me point-blank if I took the money."

"Did you?"

"No, and believe me, if I could do things over, I'd have called and visited. I'd have cleared my name eight years ago."

"Not too late to clear it," Frank said.

"It's the only way you're going to get past Beth's mother," Fisher added. "But most things don't get solved after the first forty-eight hours."

Frank laughed. "That's only murders." Looking at Joel, he said, "Why should we believe you?"

"Motive. I didn't need the money."

"You saw it and took it because it was convenient."

"I had no reason to go to my stepfather's office."

"You wanted to say goodbye."

"I was running away! You don't say goodbye if you're running away."

"Good point," Frank said.

Fisher took Joel's accountability card from the front desk and wrote something in a tiny slot. "Time to start working on your exercises."

Joel took a mat and began his stretches under Fisher's watchful eye. After a few minutes, Fisher smiled. "Your range of motion has improved. Not only that, but your movements are smooth and a bit quicker."

"I think so, too. About the only thing worrying me is that the whole time I'm bending, I'm waiting for it to hurt. I think I expect it, so I imagine I feel it."

"I doubt what you're feeling is completely your imagination. You had a serious injury. Let's add five minutes to the bike, and today we'll get you started on some lifts. First, though, the ball."

Frank Peabody usually started with the ball. Joel had wanted to laugh while watching the man strive to stay upright and bounce. A few seconds on the ball, make that a few seconds on the ball and a whole lot of minutes on the floor, made Joel appreciate what the man, fifty years his senior, was capable of.

"Don't expect it to happen all at once," Fisher said.

"I've been here a month and I keep waiting for something to happen. Either I'll start feeling one hundred percent, or I'll stiffen up again."

"You're doing great," Fisher said. "Most people,

suffering an injury like the one you endured, would kiss away any hope of competition. You were in great shape to begin with, and you didn't waste any time getting the right kind of therapy. I don't think it's going to take you six months."

Joel's mouth opened. It's what he'd been praying for. "Any chance I'll get a release form by the end of November? I can still make it to a rodeo or two."

"Maybe," Fisher said. "Depends on what happens during the next five weeks."

Five weeks was the perfect allotment. He'd promised to step in for Billy and help with the Fall Festival. After that, if Billy returned, Joel could waltz out of town with a clear conscience.

Except for the need to clear his name.

Then, too, there was Beth Armstrong, whose presence sometimes made Joel forget what was more important: the rodeo or the romance.

Chapter Thirteen

"You look nice," Linda said. "Going somewhere special on a Thursday evening?"

"Just the Fall Festival meeting," Beth replied. "We have to have everything in place tonight so we can start ordering and figuring out how many parent volunteers we need."

"You're wearing that to a plain old meeting?"

Beth looked down at her outfit. Emerald green pants and a matching jacket over a shimmering white top. Thanks to a brisk wind, whispering the promise of future snow, she wore white Danshuz shoes with just over an inch heel, which unfortunately hid her perfectly manicured toes. Granted, the outfit was new, although it had hung in a closet for over three months because she really had no cause to wear it.

"I figured it's silly of me to leave perfectly good clothes hanging in my closet and wear the same old thing."

"You mean it's silly of you to just let them hang

there when Joel's going to be at the meeting tonight and you can impress him."

Beth turned and started to march back into her bedroom. What had she been thinking?

"Stop!" Linda ordered. "You're right to wear it. You'll knock Joel's socks off. Don't change."

"I don't want to knock Joel's socks off. He can lose socks and other pieces of himself all by himself. Did you know he's going from meeting with the physical therapist three times a week to just two times a week? Do you know what that means?"

"It means when he lifts you to plant a big kiss on the willing face of yours, he won't grunt with pain or drop you."

That would be a dream come true. Dreams, however, were fleeting. "It means he's getting back on the bull and next time, instead of hurting his back, he'll break his neck."

"Statistically," Linda said sardonically, "most cowboys don't break their necks. They retire and start raising little bucking bulls."

Beth wanted to stomp her foot. Her sister knew exactly what Beth was talking about.

"He'll be like dad. He'll probably die!"

Linda put down the magazine she'd been reading. Then, she reached for the television control and turned off the program she'd been watching. "Is that what's really bothering you, this whole time? I thought you were afraid of Mom. I confess, I'm afraid of Mom. Then I believed you every time you moaned about the fact that he will leave. But the problem is, you're really afraid Joel will die?"

Beth couldn't move. She couldn't make her feet deliver her back to her bedroom and into jeans and a T-shirt, like she'd worn to every other Fall Festival meeting. Nor could she convince them to walk past her sister and out the front door.

"The fact that he has no intention of staying is huge," argued Beth. "It makes no sense investing time in something temporary."

"He's not a something," Linda said calmly. "He's a someone, a someone you've been in love with practically your whole life."

Aggravated, Beth turned and went to her bedroom to change into her regular clothes.

So she'd be comfortable at the meeting.

And, one thing for sure, if her sister had noticed her being all dressed up and nailed the exact reason why, so would their mother.

This time, even as Beth thought the words *not worth it,* she knew she was kidding herself.

Beth entered the classroom and looked around. School committees tended to be the same people every time. A few teachers and staff members and a handful of ultra-dedicated parents. Billy had been spearheading this festival since he had retired the year Mandy got sick. Besides being a fundraiser, the Fall Festival was a "best chili" contest, a cake decorating contest for kids, a used toy and book fair and various booths. It always fell on the Friday before Thanksgiving. The group, who'd already laid the groundwork, had four weeks to tie up loose ends.

Joel looked up the minute Beth walked in the room, and she realized that she'd completely wasted her time. The man didn't care what she wore. His eyes started at the top of her head and raked all the way to her feet. She felt a deliciously warm feeling flush through her body. Then, he let his gaze meander upward. Max actually had to nudge him. Luckily, Beth's mother, ensconced between the new principal and the woman in charge of the parents' group, didn't notice. She'd spent the last four weeks, since finding out Joel would be taking his stepfather's place, trying to make sure Max McClanahan really was in charge and trying to find a loophole to make sure Joel couldn't serve.

She'd failed.

All those years ago when the RC money had disappeared, no formal charges had been filed. There'd been no arrests made, restitution hadn't been given by the accused but by his brother, and now that the accused was back in town, Joel proclaimed loud and clear and to anyone who would listen that he was innocent. The school's attorney advised Beth's mother to desist.

She was desisting so much she looked ready to explode.

Beth sat down next to Mona Gabor, who leaned over and whispered, "Are you nuts? Go sit by him."

Max checked his watch, cleared his throat and stood. "Let's get this meeting on the road. Last time we met, Billy passed around the final budget. Anyone have something to add?"

For the next hour, Joel pretty much kept to himself, nodding every once in a while and sometimes pointing to something on the agenda and quietly asking a question of Max. The rest of the committee, save Beth's mother, accepted Joel as they would any last-minute volunteer.

Joel got Max's old job: the concessions.

"He'll be handling money," Beth's mom pointed out.

"With about ten other volunteers," Max responded.

"You have a problem with me handling money?" Joel asked.

Beth's mom didn't dare respond. She looked at the principal. Before he could respond, Joel suggested, in a much calmer voice than Beth expected, "Mrs. Armstrong, why don't you work concessions with me?"

Patsy Armstrong's mouth opened, but before she could protest, Mona Gabor spoke up, "I'll do your old job, Patsy. I can walk around seeing what everyone needs and restocking."

"I think it's a good idea," Max said. "Next item."

"The only thing left," Meg Peabody, the PTA secretary, said, "is coming up with a new main attraction. You guys were supposed to email me with ideas. I didn't receive a one."

"I think hiring a clown might be a good idea," Beth's mom said. "It falls well below the budget and kids will love it."

"A clown is not an attraction unless we put him on a stage," Beth opposed. "Otherwise, all he'll do is walk around and hug kids. And, since I dress up like a clown while I do face painting, it seems redundant."

"You're not funny," Mom told Beth. "We had a clown a few years ago. He was great. He also made those cute little balloons."

"And he charged the parents five dollars for each one," the man who handled ticket sales remembered. "Then, he pocketed the income, plus what we paid him. I'm only going to vote for a clown if one of us learns to twist balloons and agrees to donate the money to the school."

After about an hour of back and forth, with no decisions made and building frustration, Max asked the secretary to go back to the minutes from a year ago and see what ideas they'd put forth and rejected. Maybe one could be resurrected. She started punching keys on her laptop. Last year didn't have anything exciting. It took almost eight years of brainstorming lists before one of the suggestions earned a response from the committee.

Beth saw Joel perk up. "Who suggested a mechanical bull?" he asked.

"I believe it was Billy."

"Oh, no, not the bull," Beth's mom said quickly.

"I remember when Billy suggested it. It was the year after Joel left. Don't ask me why, since it was a bad idea, but we looked into the cost, the space needed and the insurance. Besides, kids could get hurt."

Meg Peabody, the secretary, spoke up, "Before we go on, and although I like the idea, maybe you want to consider that it wasn't just the danger like Patsy said, it was the cost. My notes say that the rental fee on a mechanical bull was almost two thousand dollars and that was eight years ago. They've probably gone up."

"Maybe not," Max said. "I don't think they're as popular."

"The kids would love it," the third grade teacher said.

"Do they make mechanical bulls kid-size?" another wanted to know.

Meg kept reading from the minutes. "Yes, they do. The reason we nixed the idea had to do with insurance purposes and the thought of making every single parent sign a release waiver before we let their child ride."

"Wouldn't whoever we rent the mechanical bull from have to carry insurance and take care of those details?" someone asked.

"Doesn't matter," Meg said. "We don't have two thousand dollars for the rental."

"You know," Joel said, "we need to be stepping away from the word *mechanical*. I know what you're all envisioning, and I think we can find something much scaled down that would make everyone happy, wannabe bull riders and worried parents. One of my buddies dropped out of the circuit five years ago and bought a place in Kansas. He's got a four-year-old. I was visiting him last year and he had this pretend bull in the barn. He'd actually used a rocking horse, but I know I could come up with something better."

"What are you thinking, Joel?" Beth was interested to hear his answer.

"I could build a contraption with no more than ropes and pulleys—more or less a combination swing-piñata—that looks like a bull and does a few more twists, jumps and sudden stops."

"That sounds doable, and it won't be so dangerous if we put rubber mats around the bull for them to land on," Max said. "This is our one-hundred-year anniversary, too, remember. We need to make this festival stand out."

"The kids would love it," the third grade teacher said again.

"Are you kidding?" Max said. "We'd want an adult-size, too. I'd ride it."

"You've ridden the real thing," Joel protested. "Why would you need to ride a fake?"

"Because," Max said wryly, "I no longer have any desire to ride the real thing. I don't want to be hobbling around like you at just thirty."

Joel laughed. "Touché."

"We only budgeted three hundred dollars for our

main attraction," the secretary put in. "I don't think we can go much higher."

"We haven't taken a vote," Mom said. "And this is something we'd have to take to the school board."

Joel didn't seem to be paying attention. "If we can get some of the materials donated, the cost will be well below three hundred dollars, plus you can keep it and use it for other years."

"Still dangerous," Beth's mom said.

"So is a pony ride," Max said, nodding slowly. "Let's take a vote. If we're in agreement, I'll go speak with the superintendent."

"I'm liking this idea more and more," said Meg. "We have all kinds of games and food, but something that lets them be a little wild, lets them pretend, I'm all for it."

"Being wild isn't something to be proud of," Mom pointed out.

"I'd rather my child be a little wild," said Meg, "than go through life afraid."

Beth almost fell off her chair. She knew, without a doubt, Meg was referring to her own children and chiding Mom about always worrying about the danger. Beth could almost hear her mother say, as she had over and over, "But somebody has to worry about the danger."

Meg, however, had taken it a step further. She'd brought up the word *afraid*.

Is that what Beth was doing? Going through life afraid?

Two nays. Mom and another volunteer. Thirteen

yeas. Beth pretended not to see the disgusted look her mother sent her way.

She'd probably get another disgusted look soon, because Beth had decided it was time to stop being afraid. Next time Joel asked her out, she was going to say yes.

"Let's go for it," Max decided. "Dad says the portion of fence Joel fixed has never been stronger. I trust him." Turning to Joel, he stipulated, "Can you make one that works for both kids and adults? Or, do we need two?"

"I can make one that would work for both."

"Good," Max said. "Count on me to be one of your crash dummies before the event."

Beth thought about the porch swing she'd shared with Joel just the other day. He'd made it. Joel wouldn't need a crash dummy. "I'll help Joel," she volunteered. "Just let me know the materials, and I'll start scavenging for donations."

"How much time do I have?" Joel asked.

"A month."

"I'll build two then."

"Twice as dangerous," Beth's mom said.

Beth felt something stir inside her. Maybe it was just anticipating saying yes the next time Joel asked her out. Or maybe it was just getting caught up in the moment. "I'll ride," she declared. "I'm looking forward to it."

Her mom raised an eyebrow. No words were necessary. The look Patsy Armstrong shot Beth told her and everyone present at the meeting something they already knew. The mechanical bull wasn't the biggest danger.

Joel was.

Chapter Fourteen

"You look nice," Linda said, coming out of the tiny bedroom that flanked the living room. "Going somewhere special?"

Those were the exact same words Linda had used yesterday, and Beth was wearing the exact same clothes. Today the words sounded so much better, and Beth intended to actually leave the house wearing her new outfit.

"I'm going to dinner with Joel so we can discuss the materials he needs to build a mechanical bull." Beth practically danced across the living room floor. If there'd have been more room, she would have. Instead, she danced into her bedroom to put on her shoes.

"Right," Linda drawled. "That's why I go on most of my dates."

Beth danced back into the dining room/office. She'd never really thought about how little room she and Linda had. Linda, mostly, wasn't home. And to Beth, the living room was just fine for the two of them. This house, built back in the thirties, was a bungalow, really. They had a tiny porch, which opened into a living room just big enough for a couch, armchair, television and two end tables. The living room led into what used to be the dining room. Instead of a table, both Beth and Linda had made the room into their office. A large desk held a computer, next to it a printer. There was a table against the other wall with some of Beth's school stuff and a bunch of painting supplies that she seldom got to use anymore. Linda had cosmetology stuff spread on the table, too.

Beth's steps slowed.

What she was looking at was a second year of sameness. They'd moved in together, the two sisters, and felt safe and comfortable.

She was too young for comfortable.

"Whatcha doing, Unca Joe?" Somewhere between Joel's arrival and his new role of Mr. Mom, Caleb had shortened his name from Joel to Joe.

"Planning dinner." Joel put the frozen pizzas on the counter and looked out the kitchen window. Jared should be coming any minute. Last night, when Joel got home from the committee meeting, Jared had been asleep. When Joel got the boys up this morning, Jared had already been out in the field.

"I yike pizza."

"Matt doesn't." Ryan entered the kitchen. The

knees of his pants were covered with grass. A few strands were in his hair. Good. He'd been helping his dad, which meant that Jared wasn't too far away.

Joel mentally kicked himself. He should have made the time to seek out Jared and fill him in about tonight's plans. "How can Matt not like pizza?"

Ryan headed for the sink and a glass of water. "He doesn't like the sauce."

This was not the best time to find out. Joel had spent the day doing therapy, buying groceries and scouring the internet, looking for ideas on how to best make a rope-and-pulley bull. Then, he'd come home—*home*—and worked on Jared's books. Through every venture, in the back of his mind, he replayed the minutes after the committee meeting when he'd managed to get to the classroom door at the same time as Beth.

"Dinner tomorrow night?"

When she answered yes, he almost didn't believe her. Especially since her mom loomed in the background, looking like she wished the floor would open up and swallow Joel whole.

And the evening would begin in just thirty minutes if only Jared would come in and agree that two frozen pizzas were the perfect Friday night meal.

"He doesn't ever eat pizza? Ever?" Joel questioned.

"Ever," came a deep-voiced answer from the doorway. Jared brushed dirt from his hands and followed Ryan's example. When he finally finished his glass of water, he added, "We've even taken him into Des

Moines and to one of those pizza places that has all the talking animals and games and such. He ate the crust."

At that moment, Jared noted the pizza boxes on the counter. "Just make Matt a hot dog," he suggested.

Stricken, Joel looked at the frozen pizzas.

"You're dressed up," Jared noted. "Want to tell me something, like why you've actually set out something I can prepare and why the thought of adding a hot dog to the mix causes such panic?"

"I have a date with Beth tonight."

"Matt's teacher!" Ryan burst out.

"You always did take chances." To Joel's surprise, Jared sounded impressed.

"You've been taking some, too," Joel said. "I balanced the books today. The farmer's market stand you put up is really bringing in some money."

"We just might end up in the black," Jared agreed. "What time is your date?"

Joel looked at his watch. "Twenty minutes."

"Get out of here," Jared urged. "I can manage to add hot dogs to the menu."

As Joel hurried out of the kitchen and through the living room, he heard the phone ring. "If that's Beth, tell her I'm going to be a few minutes late."

Joel made it to the front door, when he heard Caleb squeal "Grandpa!" and stopped in his tracks.

Asking Billy a few questions was about the only thing that could keep Joel from hurrying out the door.

* * *

Chauncy's was a steak house ten miles from Roanoke's city limits. It was housed in a converted barn owned by the wealthiest family in the area.

They just kept on getting wealthier while the rest of the area's farmers did things like open farmer's markets and try planting alternative crops, just to get by.

"How long has this been here?" Joel asked, exiting his truck and going around to help Beth.

"Five years? Susan had her wedding reception here two years ago."

A wagon, loaded with hay and led by a horse, waited at the end of a line of cars. "Would you rather walk so you don't get hay on your clothes?" Joel asked.

"And miss the fun? Are you kidding?"

Joel put both hands on her waist and gave her a boost up into the wagon. She felt warm and alluring. Settling on a bale of hay, she scooted over so he could have room. After a few minutes, they were deposited at the barn, where country music could already be heard. They waited in a crowd of about ten, all of whom greeted them, looking askance at Joel, before they were seated. Finally, the hostess came back and led Joel and Beth to a table, in a dark corner, far away from the band. "How many daughters does Frank Peabody have?" Joel asked.

"Two," Beth replied. "Amanda's a granddaughter."

"Meg's his daughter?"

A waitress brought over two glasses of water and some bread. "Need a minute?"

"Yes."

For a few seconds, they looked at the menu. While Joel liked the intimacy of the dark corner, he also wished for bright lights. He didn't want her glorious hair to be muted in deep shadows. He wanted to see every smile, every nod, and maybe, if he got lucky, she'd even wink again like she'd done that first Sunday at church.

Stealing a glance at her, he wondered what she was thinking. She'd made the comment that she'd agreed to the date so they could talk about the pretend bull's materials, but she wasn't dressed like she wanted to talk ropes, pulleys and hooks.

She was dressed like she wanted to talk holding hands, late night walks and cuddling.

He was thinking like a man in love, and this was only the first date.

"You ready?"

"I am."

She ordered an impressive amount of food for such a small woman and when the waitress walked away, she smiled at him. Oh, he was definitely feeling something beyond just common attraction.

"So, did you have physical therapy today?"

"I did, and the news is still good. By the way, that's why I asked about the Peabody girl. You know, Frank Peabody, the old mailman, goes there. He and I get along pretty good."

Beth chuckled. "He gets along with everyone. My mom says Meg used to make him help out at school events. Plus, he comes and visits our classrooms at least once a year and does a little skit about what happens to a letter after it's mailed."

"I've been asking him questions. He's been telling me about the Fall Festival eight years ago. He remembers some pretty interesting things."

"I hope you figure out what really happened."

"He's also told me some things about when my parents were young."

"Tell me some of them." Beth leaned forward, all interest.

"He said that my mom's mother, my grandma who I never met, didn't like my dad. At all."

"Does he know why?"

"She thought my dad and his parents were old sticks-in-the-mud. That's a direct quote. She was afraid my mom would wind up stuck on the farm and never have any fun."

"Mandy said the farm was great fun. She especially enjoyed sitting in the backyard with the boys and watching them play in the dirt."

"My mom used to do that with us, too," Joel said. "Only, I remember her sitting there helping us make car tracks and haul dirt."

"I think the saddest day in Mandy's life was when she went from doing that exact same thing to having to watch. After she got sick, she didn't move so easily."

"You miss her."

"Every day. She was my best friend. I'm lucky, I have my sisters, but Mandy never judged like they do. I never heard her say, 'Beth, go ahead and get dirty. Beth, you've got to stand up to Mom. Beth, it's okay to read a book instead of going roller-skating.' Friends like that are rare," Beth finished.

The waitress came back with salads.

"She thought the world of Billy," Beth continued, after taking a few bites. "She always said he was the best father-in-law in the world."

"Good, that means you completely understand why I had to be late."

"I'm glad Billy finally called. What all did he say?"

"He's in Handfast, Kansas. Ever heard of it?"

"No, and it sounds like a made up name."

"It's real. Jared got out the atlas so he could show the kids. Billy's visiting friends."

"When is he coming home?"

"I told him that I expected to have a doctor's release right after the Fall Festival. I'm going to start small. My ultimate goal, unless something happens, is to head to Vegas and watch the championships the first ten days in December. I'll probably miss the November Mesquite Holiday Rodeo since I've volunteered to do the Fall Festival. But there's the Mesquite Holiday Rodeo at the end of December in Dallas. I think I can scrape together the entry fee."

"So," Beth said, "you'll be here another month at least."

"Oh, now that I'm home and needed, I'm not really

going away. I'm going to make this home base. I have to be sensible. Mesquite will show me if I still have the right stuff."

"What does Jared say?"

"Jared's too busy trying to keep his family together to worry about whether or not I have the right stuff."

"No, I mean about you coming and going."

"Right now he's just happy that I'm here. He's also pretty impressed that I had the guts to ask you out. Tell me, are all the guys in town afraid to ask you out because of your mother?"

"Sometimes I think so," Beth admitted. "Truly, though, she just wants what is best for us."

"I can understand that."

Their food arrived. Joel looked across at her and wondered just how much courage it took for her to go against her mother. She had a college degree, a good job and the world at her fingertips.

But could his world be hers?

"You want to pray?" she asked, reaching across to take his hand.

Just one touch convinced him. He was willing to change for her.

Joel didn't really want to thank his Heavenly Father for the good meal they were about to partake of. And Joel had already said plenty of prayers concerning his health. But until this minute, Joel hadn't realized how much he needed prayer. With Beth, he was going to need all the help he could get.

Quickly, out loud, Joel thanked God for their meal.

After a few bites, to Joel's surprise, Beth continued with their earlier topic: her mother versus Joel.

"I think it's more your profession than anything else," she said. "Mom, well, Mom never got over my dad's death. She doesn't want us to suffer like she did."

"I know your dad died in a rock climbing accident. What exactly happened? Or does it bother you to talk about it?"

"I don't even remember him. Mom certainly doesn't talk about him. He was a truck driver. Linda says he'd leave early in the morning and drive all the way to Omaha. There, he'd meet another truck driver and they'd exchange cargo. He'd come home. He worked twelve hours a day, three days a week. Because he had extra time, he made money on the side by taking climbers out to places like Indian Bluffs. A few times, he even traveled to South Dakota or Illinois. Funny thing is, the day he fell, he wasn't even working. He was alone. He was there because he wanted to have fun. After that, my sisters tell me that fun left our house completely. Mom even took down every picture that had him in it."

"We have a big portrait in the living room of my parents and Jared and me. I never thought about whether it bothered Mom while she was still alive. Or even if it bothered Billy."

"I think it's good you guys left it up. The only thing I know of my father is from what Linda re-

members. She says he was lots of fun. He'd chase
them all around the house, sometimes wearing a
monster hat. I guess he taught both Linda and Susan
to climb trees when they were about three. Susan
broke her arm falling out of one. Linda even had a
skateboard when she was not yet six. I was lucky to
get the training wheels off my bike. I sure felt his absence. It shadowed every move, every decision my
mother made."

"I can't even imagine growing up not knowing my
dad. He was great. Losing him was tough."

"Yeah, and then you wound up with Billy," Beth
said. "I think I like how your mom handled loss
better than how my mom did. But, hey, let's change
the topic. This is a little too deep for a first…"

"First date?"

"We're going to talk about the rope-and-pulley
bull, remember?"

"Sure, this is a perfect backdrop for that conversation. Did you bring any paper to take notes on?"

She laughed. "You win. What else do you want to
talk about?"

He finished the last bite of his baked potato and
shook his fork at her. "Hmm, do you want to know
what I've been doing besides trying to get a date with
you?"

"I'm glad you were persistent."

Not as glad as he was. Hopefully she was open to

his continued persistence, because he wanted this date to be the first of many.

"I'm getting to know my nephews. Ryan and Caleb are easy. Matt is taking some time."

"He's very sensitive. I do think, however, that having you here has been good. He's been forced to come out of his shell. He's speaking up more at school."

"That's good to know. He's going to help me tomorrow out at Solitaire's Market. Ryan usually does, but he has a birthday party to attend."

"Don't do things for him," Beth advised. "Let him help. He needs to feel needed."

"Something else I've decided to do is figure out what really happened to the money that disappeared the night I left."

"What have you discovered so far?"

"Not much. Last night, when Meg Peabody was shuffling through the minutes going back multiple years, I decided to ask her for the minutes from eight years ago. She's promised to get me copies."

"Good thinking."

"The main reason I was late tonight," Joel said, "wasn't just because I needed to talk to Billy about the things we're doing now that he's gone. I wanted to talk about the night the money disappeared. I didn't discover anything new. He'd already told me about working that night, about gathering up the money and putting it in the office so they could count it the next morning."

"Who was the treasurer back then?"

"He's another reason why I know the timing is good. The treasurer was my friend Frank Peabody. I started asking him questions this morning during therapy. He's promised to try to remember if anything unusual happened that night. Before, during or after."

"Does Jared remember anything?"

"They left early. He was at the festival with Mandy and Ryan."

"Ryan would have been an infant."

"Just a few months old, which is why Jared was home at eight that night."

"Who else could you ask?"

"If I can get up the courage, I thought I'd ask your mother."

"She certainly knows everything that happens at church, at the school and in all our lives. Always has."

"That's what Billy said, too," Joel agreed. They finished the last of their meal. Joel paid the check with money he'd gotten from Jared, who said Joel more than deserved it, and then he guided Beth out the door.

It took a minute for the hay wagon to return from dropping off other people. This time, when he went to help Beth up and into the wagon's bed, he held on for a minute, not wanting to release her. She must have felt the same way, because the moment she got her footing, she turned to him and gave him a smile full of promises.

Chapter Fifteen

Saturday morning, so bright and early that the nephews didn't get a chance to creep into his room with questions and comments, Joel started setting up Solitaire's Market by opening windows and airing out the structure. Then he checked his watch again. It was twenty-six hours and fourteen minutes until he'd see Beth again. He'd spend at least eight of them in this structure because Jared liked to keep it open until four.

This was Solitaire Market's final weekend. The day after tomorrow was the night when pumpkins were a necessity, and Jared was hoping for a boom in business. Jared was already in a good mood, thanks to warm temperatures, sunny skies and moderate winds. He was busy with fertilization.

Joel, of course, much preferred the role of storekeeper. The hardest part of it was the setup. He attached the minitrailer to the all-terrain vehicle that had seen better days and fetched the last of the pumpkins and gourds. After arranging them in the outside stalls, Joel got the last of the Indian corn.

In truth, Solitaire's Market gave Joel something productive to do. Plus, to his surprise, he liked running the store. It was tiny by most standards, just a prefab one-room structure his brother and Billy had built adjacent to the road.

If Joel were to stick around, and he intended to, he'd convince Jared the place needed a tiny parking lot. If it looked more like a store, they'd entice more people to make the drive out from town. Then, too, Joel wanted a hay bale maze. Enough kids came with their parents. At a dollar or two a pop, it would be profit with little overhead. Joel had a few other ideas, but Jared wasn't yet at the point where he wanted to listen to a little brother's long-term ideas, especially the little brother who'd wanted no part of Solitaire Farm just eight years ago.

Ryan had helped last week. He was a natural and actually liked helping people. His favorite thing to do was wave people in and then encourage them to buy some of the different flavored peppermint sticks Jared was smart enough to stock. Apparently, Billy paid one peppermint stick for every ten Ryan helped sell: a win-win arrangement. Ryan had also figured out that helping to carry bags to the cars often earned him a quarter tip.

Joel had just wiped off the counter, when Matt ventured in. If ever there were a child who didn't want to be a storekeeper's assistant, it was Matt.

Caleb would have been a better choice. He'd sell a dozen peppermint sticks just by announcing, "I yike them."

Matt opened the door to the structure, didn't greet Joel, threw his backpack on the floor and promptly sat on a chair behind the checkout counter. Before Joel could even suggest that he sweep the floor or at least flip over the Open sign, Matt put his head down.

"You tired?" Joel asked.

Without looking up, Matt shook his head no.

"You ever help out here before?"

Again the negative.

An hour later, Matt was pretty much in the same position. Maybe he'd scooted his chair a half inch to the side in order to make sure Joel didn't get too close while ringing up a customer.

Since they'd only had three customers, the interaction between uncle and nephew was fleeting. The interaction between customer and nephew had been zero.

"What's in the backpack?" Joel asked.

Matt didn't answer.

Joel pulled his cell phone from his pocket and hit a button.

Matt's head jerked up. "Who are you calling?"

"Your dad. I figure he'll have some ideas on how to get you motivated."

"No!" Matt sounded a bit panicked, which was exactly what Joel wanted.

Joel hung up.

"I didn't finish my homework last night," Matt admitted. "Dad said I should finish it today if I had time. He said you would help me."

Sounds like something Jared would do.

"I don't want your help," Matt said.

Picking up his nephew's yellow superhero backpack, Joel fished out the red folder that carried homework and notes back and forth from school. Inside the folder was Friday's newsletter. Jared should have read it last night. Basically, it said that the students were doing great and improving. It listed the letter *K* as the letter of the week. It also asked for parent volunteers for the upcoming Fall Festival. There were four other papers. Two were *J* handwriting papers. They weren't marked as homework. Another was a page that had a jack-in-the-box picture. Kids were instructed to cut out the pictures that began with *J*. The page looked like it hadn't been touched. The only page that had the word *homework* on it simply contained flash-card words and instructions to practice.

"Do you do flash cards at school?"

Matt shrugged.

Joel thought about whipping out his cell phone and threatening to call Jared again, but that would be too easy. Besides, Joel knew the best person for the job. Pulling out his cell phone again, he hit a number that he fully intended to put on his speed-dial.

"Hi, Beth."

* * *

It felt good to be heading for Solitaire Farm again, and this time in a role she was comfortable with: beloved friend, quasi family member.

It's how she felt when Mandy was alive. She liked feeling that way with Joel, for now, although eventually she definitely wanted more.

When she arrived, the market had three cars parked out in front. Two were pulling out to leave. Joel and another man were standing next to the remaining vehicle. Beth parked next to it and hopped out.

"Hey, Beth," Frank Peabody greeted. "I thought I'd mosey on over and pick up some Indian corn. The wife likes to decorate with it during the holidays. Me, I think it's a waste of time and money."

"Hello, Mr. Peabody. You ready to come speak to my class next month about being a postal worker?"

"Just tell me when. You gonna have your young man come talk about being a bull rider?"

"He's not my young man," Beth protested, trying not to smile.

"You forget," Mr. Peabody said, "that I'm in therapy with him three times a week."

"Two times a week now," Joel interrupted.

Mr. Peabody paid him no mind. "There's only so much talking you can do about the Iowa weather. He's been talking about you off and on for three weeks. About time you said yes when he asked you out."

"Where's Matt?" Beth changed the subject.

Both men pointed inside the structure. Beth walked over and peeked through the open window. Matt was fast asleep in a chair with his head on the counter.

What she didn't tell them was that he often fell asleep at school, too. Beth mentally kicked herself. With the arrival of Joel, she'd been distracted. Matt had to be her biggest concern. He needed help.

And, luckily, it looked like Joel was willing to be right there beside her giving it.

After a few more moments of watching Matt sleep, noticing how peaceful he looked, she joined Joel as he waited for Mr. Peabody to gather up three envelopes.

"This one," Mr. Peabody said, "contains copies of the treasury report for the three years I kept the books. Then, this one contains my daughter's minutes going back ten years. I took a quick look, and the money you were accused of taking wasn't the first money to go missing. This last envelope has the only two articles that the *Roanoke Globe* published about the theft."

Beth peered over Joel's shoulder as he took two tiny newspaper articles and read them. They finished at the same time.

Joel looked at Beth. "I didn't know your mother was a witness to my leaving the 'darkened school hallway,'" he quoted the exact words from the longer article.

"I didn't, either."

"Patsy's always watching out for the school," Mr. Peabody said. "She caught two teenagers from the next town over breaking in and stealing computers just two years ago. She saved the district thousands of dollars. Those kids had already stolen computers just a month earlier. They had just been replaced."

"Nervy to come back to the same place," Joel remarked.

"Teenagers aren't always the sharpest pencils in the pack." Mr. Peabody opened his driver's side door and got in.

"Thanks." Joel held up the envelopes. "I appreciate the help. You need any of this back?"

"No, I made copies of the PTA stuff. It's all public record. As for the newspaper articles, I only had them because my youngest daughter was the reporter who wrote the stories. Wife keeps two of everything in a scrapbook."

"I need to talk to his youngest daughter," Joel said, watching as Mr. Peabody drove away.

"You want me to talk to my mother?" Beth offered, moving over to stand next to him.

"No, I'll find the time to talk to her."

"Before or after she finds out you took me on a date?"

"You mean she doesn't know?"

"I haven't told her, and Linda claims to be scared to. I'm not sure Susan knows yet. I mean, it just happened last night. Even in Roanoke, it takes a while for news to make the front page."

"You're right," Joel said. "This is Roanoke. She knows."

"She knows," Beth agreed.

It took Joel only a moment to reach over and draw Beth even closer than she already was. "Let's give her something else to worry about," he suggested.

Then he kissed her.

To Joel's way of thinking, the kiss didn't last near long enough because a loud noise inside Solitaire's Market let them know Matt was awake and had fallen off his chair.

After picking up and brushing off the embarrassed five-year-old, Joel looked around the market. "We can probably start cleaning up. Jared says this is the last day since we're down to just three pumpkins."

He didn't get to continue. Beth took charge, claiming, "I helped out when Jared was taking care of Mandy at the end."

"I don't remember that," Matt said.

"You were three, just Caleb's age."

Matt looked somewhat impressed, impressed enough that he willingly pitched in and asked all kinds of questions about those long-ago days. After about three hours of grunt work, the place was cleaned, put away and locked up. Solitaire's Market was now closed for the season. Matt helped carry the last of the produce to the minitrailer hitched to the ATV.

"Maybe," Matt suggested shyly, "we can decorate one of the pumpkins."

"Decorate one of the pumpkins?" Joel let the words trail off. What kind of uncle was he? The boys had been talking about what was happening after evening services tomorrow for weeks. But Billy hadn't mentioned it in his list of things to do. And, typical of a distracted father and a bachelor uncle, both men had let the boys' jabbering go in one ear and out the other.

"We can put it in the back of your truck tomorrow after service, during Trunk or Treat. We can decorate as long as we do nice things." For being the least talkative nephew, Matt was suddenly full of ideas.

"It's not a bad idea," Beth sided with Matt. "I'm helping serve for the picnic."

Now, the picnic Joel had taken note of, free food and lots of it. He'd just missed thinking about what to do for the kids' portion of the event.

"We have three pumpkins," Joel noted, "and I have three nephews."

Matt screwed up his face, quickly seeing where this was going. "Caleb might be too little."

"Maybe Beth can stay and help Caleb." Finally, Joel had a suggestion of his own. "After all, she still needs to help you with your homework."

"Just try to get rid of me," Beth responded.

Back at the farm, Beth sat in the kitchen and helped Matt with his homework. Ryan received extra help—somewhat needed, not necessarily wanted—

by default. The promise of pumpkin decorating seemed to counterbalance the idea of extra work. Then, at suppertime, Beth taught Joel how to make homemade meat loaf and mashed potatoes. Who knew cooking was so much fun?

Jared walked in about five minutes before the meal was ready. He took in the boys still sitting at the table working on school papers, the aroma of good food and Beth's presence with unusual good grace. "Looks like you've been having fun."

"And there's more to come," Beth promised.

She was telling the truth. Soon three pumpkins sat waiting for tomorrow's adventure at church. Jared and Ryan had created a Star Wars pumpkin. Joel and Matt came up with a Spider-Man pumpkin. Beth and Caleb, not to be left out, designed a train pumpkin.

Of course, it looked more like the magical carriage from Cinderella, but Caleb didn't seem to mind.

Afterward, Jared herded the boys into their baths and Joel and Beth headed back to the swing. Exhausted, Joel leaned back and Beth rested against him as he nudged the swing back and forth.

"You tired?" he asked.

"Deliciously so."

Only a female could word it quite so accurately.

"That's the happiest I've seen Matt in almost a year."

"I agree." The screen door creaked open and Jared stepped out.

"You done with baths already?" Joel asked.

"Caleb and Matt fell asleep before I could get them in the bath. I tucked them into bed. Ryan's old enough to take care of himself, although he's indignant that he has to take a bath." Jared sat in the old rocker that had been their grandmother's. "Thanks, Beth. My kids had a full day."

"You're welcome. I didn't realize how much I missed helping with Solitaire's Market. Call me anytime."

"How much did you bring in?" Jared asked.

"One hundred twelve dollars and some change. All that's left is Indian corn."

"I'll take it," Beth volunteered. "I've an art project I've been wanting to do with my class. How much?"

"It's yours. Consider it payment for helping out with the market."

Beth smiled. "Thanks! Joel, you can bring it to school Monday morning."

"Frank Peabody came by," Joel told Jared. "He brought me some of the PTA records from the time the money went missing. He also brought a couple of newspaper articles."

"I didn't even bother to look at them way back then," Jared admitted. "I was too mad. Did they tell you anything new?"

"No, not really."

Joel tightened his grip around Beth's shoulders. "It's not only that I want to clear my name, but Jared's due some money. He reimbursed the PTA so they wouldn't file charges against me."

"I wish I'd waited," Jared admitted. "Maybe then, the real thief would have been caught."

"It's a lot of money," Beth admitted. "My mom still talks about how much. We've not come near that amount the last few years."

"Eight years ago the economy hadn't quite tanked yet," Jared said. "Your mom was so appalled," he added. "I remember her poking me in the chest and saying I should have controlled Joel better. As if I had any control over him."

"Why did you choose that night to leave?" Beth asked, making Joel feel like he never wanted to leave again.

He stopped pushing the swing, feeling dizzy from Beth's proximity and a little hesitant to show his vulnerability to his brother.

"I think it was standing at the festival and watching you over by the picnic tables."

"Me?" Jared asked.

"You, Mandy, little Ryan and Billy. You took over one end. Mandy was holding Ryan, and you were right next to him. Billy sat across from you with the kid carrier by him."

"So?"

"There was no room for me."

Jared didn't say anything but a look of understanding passed over his face before he stood up.

"I'd better check on Ryan," he said, disappearing into the house.

Beth nuzzled her head against Joel's shoulder and he began to push the swing again, feeling light, as though relieved of a heavy burden.

Chapter Sixteen

"There's not a chance I'm riding with you," Linda said, peeking into Beth's bedroom on Sunday morning. "Unless, of course, you tell me that Mom called and she's not going to church today."

Beth closed her eyes. She'd gotten home at close to eleven. She'd stayed up past midnight prepping for her Sunday school class, and now she'd overslept. None of these things made this morning any easier, so there was no way she was taking on Mom alone. "Oh, yes, you're coming with me. Is it possible that Mom hasn't heard?"

"Nope," Linda replied. "Not a chance. Yesterday, every customer I had was talking about you and Joel."

Beth didn't bother to respond. Rolling out of bed and feeling sluggish was new to her. She usually woke well before her alarm clock, ate a leisurely breakfast, put on the clothes she'd selected the night before and then headed out the door after grabbing the bag she'd packed the previous evening.

This morning, the bag was the only thing ready.

By skipping breakfast, Beth would have an extra minute to make sure she looked good, and she definitely wanted to look good—a certain cowboy was sure to notice. "Why didn't you wake me sooner?"

Linda stepped into the bedroom. Still in her pajamas, her hair a mess, she accused, "You always wake *me* up."

Thirty minutes later, Beth pulled up in front of her mother's house. Patsy Armstrong was already on the porch, checking her watch and waiting. Beth was five minutes late.

Linda hopped out of the passenger seat, left the door open and got in the back. Patsy took her place.

"Sorry, Mom," Beth said. "Time got away from us this morning."

"Us?" Linda said from the backseat.

Beth affirmed, "From me." As soon as her mother put on her seat belt, Beth tapped the gas pedal.

"I wasn't waiting long," Mom said. "And it's a nice day."

If Linda had been in the front seat, Beth could have sent a panicked look. Mom was being nice, especially considering Thursday night's meeting, when Beth didn't vote the same way. Dreading Mom finding out was almost worse than Mom already knowing. And the drive to the church would certainly qualify as a good time to share. If Beth didn't say something about this past weekend with Joel,

Mom would tell her, "The only things you need to hide are the things you're ashamed of."

"What'd you do this weekend, Mom?" Linda asked from the backseat.

"Yesterday, I spent all day at the church making caramel apples. After that, I went to the hospital to visit a friend. Another friend showed up, so I stayed and ate at the hospital cafeteria with her."

"I worked," Linda said brightly. "We were busy all day. About five girls came in and asked me to dye their hair black and white."

Mom shook her head.

"Then," Linda added, "at least two girls wanted their hair electric blue."

Mom turned, so she was facing Beth. "What did you do this weekend?"

"She's got something neat planned for her Bible school class," Linda chirped from the backseat. "I saw her putting together this—"

"Beth can answer on her own," Mom said patiently.

The church was just two blocks ahead. Just two blocks until safety. But, sometimes, especially when a questioning mother was involved, two blocks might as well be two miles, two states or two continents. "I had a date Friday night, and I actually worked yesterday."

Mom didn't respond, which told Beth that Mom easily guessed who her date was.

"What kind of work?"

"We closed down Solitaire's Market. Then I helped Matt and Ryan with their homework."

"Well, you always liked pitching in at Solitaire's Market. I hear that Joel's coming through therapy fine and will be leaving us soon."

No need to tell Mom that Joel had already decided to make Roanoke his home base. Maybe if Mom thought he'd be disappearing soon, Beth could have a little breathing room and start figuring out ways to change her mother's mind about disapproving of him.

Beth had certainly changed her mind. "He's feeling much better. Did you know he's made a cradle for Susan? It's beautiful."

"I didn't know that," Linda said helpfully.

"And you should see him with his nephews. Yesterday, Matt even smiled. And Ryan—"

"I know," Mom said. "He's picking them up, doing homework with them and calling you for help."

"Mandy was my best friend," Beth said, turning into the parking lot. "I've wanted to pitch in and help for a long time."

Mom stopped looking at Beth and instead stared out the window. "I think I'd rather you get involved with Jared. He's the more responsible of the two brothers."

In the backseat, Linda gasped.

"No, no, no," Mom protested. "I'm not suggesting it. I know that every time you look at him you think of Mandy. I'm just saying, nothing good ever came from Joel."

"Well," Linda said, "look at that."

Just two vehicles down, the passenger side door of Billy Staples's minivan opened and Joel, dressed in his Sunday best and carrying three large bags of potato chips, got out.

"That's what a bachelor brings to a picnic," said Linda.

"And look," Beth said, "he brought something even better than food."

The driver's side door of the minivan opened and Jared McCreedy stepped out.

Matt didn't want to attend Bible class. He wanted to stay with his father. Beth shooed them out of the classroom and down to the meeting room where doughnuts, coffee and fellowship awaited. Truly, Jared's attendance today was reason enough for a five-year-old to attend one of the adult classes.

"I'll stay in class with you," Caleb volunteered. "I'm big 'nuff. I'll even skip the doughnut."

"Me, too," Joel said. "I'm getting used to these little chairs."

"Soon," Beth promised Caleb. "Soon, you'll be in kindergarten." She aimed a stern look at Joel. "As for you, stay with your brother. Make sure he doesn't take one look at this crowd, change his mind and decide to make a quick getaway."

"He won't be changing his mind. You should have

seen how happy the boys were this morning. For a moment, I thought Jared might cry."

"Crying would do him good. He didn't shed a tear after Mandy died."

Before Joel could say anything more, two pint-size dynamos shot past and into seats. Both were arguing about why they didn't have their verses memorized.

"Hmm," Beth said. "Maybe your staying would be a good idea. With kids already showing up, I doubt I'll get down to the fellowship hall to socialize."

With Caleb in tow and a quick bow, Joel backed out of the room and took off down the hall after his brother. "Chicken," Beth called.

Soon more than twenty pupils were seated at the large table and Beth truly was wishing for help. Her average attendance was between eight and ten. Some of the students were first timers, lured by the promise of Trunk and Treat and sporting I'm a Visitor name badges. They were all full of spit and vinegar. So much so that Beth only made it through half of her lesson. Many of the newcomers had never heard of Moses, but thought taking a ride in a reed basket in a river sounded like great fun. When the five-minute warning bell rang, Beth let out a sigh of relief.

Finally, after straightening up the classroom, she joined a crowd of people heading toward the auditorium. Looking around, she tried to find Joel. He should be easy to spot. At six foot, he was taller than most of the Roanoke men. Jared was a good inch taller than that. Maybe they were already seated.

Before she found him, her mother waved.

Well, if Beth had sat with Joel, there'd have been plenty of questions after and not just from her mother. Sitting with a guy—especially one as handsome as Joel—pretty much gave the congregation permission to say, "Should we be planning a shower?"

Mom sat in her usual spot, just a few pews back from the pulpit.

"Where's Linda?" Beth asked, scooting past a family of four and plopping down next to her mother.

"Lost in the crowd, probably," Mom said. "I hope some of these people return next week when it's just a regular service."

"Even if we get just one, we've done something."

Her mother smiled, happy to hear repeated what she'd said so often to her offspring.

Her mother wasn't smiling a few hours later after Trunk and Treat ended. Jared had loaded his brood into the minivan and taken them home after three hours of picnicking. Joel claimed he stayed around to help, but it was pretty obvious to everyone that Joel stuck around to bother Beth.

Never had being bothered felt so good.

Now Joel sat in the front seat of Beth's car while Beth's mother and Linda were in the back.

"So if we head to Townley after dropping your mom off," Joel said, either oblivious to Beth's mother or pretending to ignore her, "we can pick up the hooks that were donated for the mechanical bull and get back here in time for evening service."

"Two hours?" Mom queried. "Townley's a good hour away."

"Not much traffic on Sunday, Mom," Beth said. "We'll be okay."

"We can always attend evening services there if we run late."

"Shouldn't you pick those things up in your truck?" Mom suggested. "After all, you don't want to dirty Beth's car."

"We can stop by the farm and trade off vehicles," Joel agreed.

"We'll just put a blanket down," Beth said, "if it all doesn't fit in the trunk."

"I'm sure glad you're going," Joel teased. "Remember, I can't do any heavy lifting."

Beth looked in the rearview mirror. Her mother wasn't laughing.

The next Saturday, Beth and Joel drove around Roanoke picking up two fifty-five-gallon canisters and an old saddle that Beth had managed to get donated.

Matt accompanied them. He wasn't the happiest child, at least not while he sat in the backseat. He came alive when they got to the junkyard to pick up a length of rope. For a kid who didn't like to get dirty, he seemed more than fascinated with the amount of human castoffs.

Yet, even with a look of wistfulness on his face, he wouldn't venture past the junkyard office.

Speaking of someone who didn't usually get dirty, Beth spent the late afternoon and early evening helping with the bull. When Jared called them in for supper, she had black smudges on her face, and she'd broken two fingernails.

"You look too happy, Miss Armstrong," Matt complained.

"I don't just *look* happy," Beth told him. "I am happy."

Matt paused, his face scrunching up, and finally he admitted, "I'm kinda happy, too." Then, as if the declaration might get him in trouble, he bolted for his room. His father had to tickle him and then carry him down the stairs to entice him to yet another meal of hot dogs and potato chips.

Joel took his seat, the one Billy used to occupy, and automatically handed Matt the ketchup while Jared took the bun away from Caleb because the three-year-old would never eat it. "I'm the better cook," Joel bragged.

"Especially when I'm helping you," Beth added.

She continued the conversation after church the next day, Sunday, as they worked together to make a noon meal. The meat loaf and mashed potatoes were a hit and even Caleb cleaned his plate.

Jared added a second helping to his plate. "If I'd known the food was going to get better, I'd have been more welcoming when Joel first arrived."

Even the three boys went silent, for just a moment, before returning to discussions of who'd gotten in trouble this morning at church, who they wanted to invite over to play and what they wanted to do for the rest of the afternoon.

It wasn't exactly an *I forgive you,* Joel thought, but it was good enough.

The warm look Beth shot him made it even better.

Later, when they'd returned from evening service and after the boys were in bed, Jared paused from his nightly ritual of walking through the house picking things up, turning off the lights and making sure all the doors were locked. He came and sat down at the kitchen table, where Joel was again looking over the plans for the mechanical bull.

"You worried?" Jared asked.

"If it wasn't for Beth's mother expecting me to fail, I'd already have the thing built."

Jared gave a half snort. "Don't let her get your goat. It's something besides you that's made her so unhappy."

"Why do you say that?"

"I just remember her from growing up. When Mandy and I got married, Mrs. Armstrong told Mandy that she should go to college and get a good job because farming didn't bring in any money. And she's the one who gave your name to the papers when the money went missing. I was just going to replace it and forget about it."

"Beth says that after her dad died, her mother pretty much stopped living."

Jared nodded slowly and reached for the bowl of grapes, a late night snack that Caleb hadn't finished. He picked one up, looked at it and then put it back in the bowl before pushing the whole thing away. "That's a good way to put it. Stopped living. And once you decide to stop living, it pretty much becomes habit."

What Jared didn't say was how good it felt that he'd started living again. That was okay. Joel could see it. And suddenly, Joel felt sorry for Patsy Armstrong, who didn't know and might never know.

Jared stood, carefully pushing back his chair and picking up Caleb's bowl to put in the sink. He paused halfway to the sink as if struggling to decide if he wanted to turn back or if he wanted to go forward. After a moment, he took the last few steps to the sink. "Tonight," he said so softly that Joel had to strain to hear him, "was the first night I didn't resent that someone else was sitting where Mandy used to sit."

Chapter Seventeen

Thursday morning dawned silver gray, gloomy and quiet. It took a moment for Joel to realize that it was the silence that awakened him. He opened one eye and glanced at the clock. After nine o'clock! He opened his other eye before rolling to a sitting position. Truthfully, he couldn't remember the last time he'd been home alone.

Jared had loaded the kids up early this morning—somehow doing it without disturbing Joel—and was probably still in route to Council Bluffs in honor of Veteran's Day. Mandy's folks lived there, and she had an elderly uncle who would be receiving some sort of award.

Jared had called Mandy's folks late last night after giving Joel a few last-minute ideas about the rope-and-pulley bull. In the quiet house, Joel had overheard enough of the conversation to realize that Jared and the kids had been invited to the event weeks ago and Jared had said no. Joel could tell from the one-sided conversation that Jared's changing his mind was cause for celebration.

Joel understood their elation. Jared had changed his mind about a lot of things lately, and the changes were for the better.

First thing Joel did was take a shower without hearing, "Unca Joe, I need in!" After that, he spent a few minutes on the porch, just breathing, thinking about what he and Beth would do the next time they got together, and thanking God for all the changes in his life. After a quick breakfast, he did a few of the floor exercises that Fisher suggested.

Funny how thoughts of rehabilitation came last. Just a month ago, that would have been his only consideration.

He finished his exercises, did what few chores Jared had left for him and then headed for the kitchen and a snack. After grabbing an apple and pouring himself a glass of milk, Joel took down the calendar that hung on the wall next to the back door to see what was coming up. Flipping through it, he realized just how faithful Billy was to detail. Every responsibility was written down, complete with times. It was early November. This calendar year neared the end. Only seven weeks left until the New Year, and Joel wondered if Billy would be back in time to start preparing for Christmas.

Joel skimmed backward to the day he had arrived and had messed up the typical routine of the

McCreedy clan. Yes, Billy had written things such as *Joel gets out of hospital* and *Joel starts physical therapy*.

Years ago Joel's mom had urged her younger son, "You'd be wise to watch him." She'd followed that with, "Gaining a few of Billy's traits will serve you well in life."

Back then, Joel hadn't understood what she was saying; he understood her now.

Today was Thursday. What had Billy typically done on Thursdays? Thoughtfully, starting in January, Joel studied each and every month.

When this calendar started, Mandy had still been alive. Doctor visits had been the family norm. Billy hadn't recorded the exact day she died. Maybe it had been too hard for him to write it down, record it where it would never go away, remind him of losing Abigail.

There were also family birthdays he'd missed and the town celebrations. Those were the big things. Billy wrote down lots of small things, too. Getting the boys to school was a given. Billy didn't write that down. Hmm, Billy, as a church elder, had done hospital visits. The church bulletin mentioned at least two people who were hospitalized. Joel knew one of them and doubted he'd know what hit him if Joel suddenly showed up and asked, "How ya doing?"

What else had Billy done?

Take flowers to Abigail's grave.

Mom's grave? Joel had been there exactly once, more than eight years ago. The day they buried her.

An uncomfortable feeling settled in the pit of Joel's stomach. There were so many mistakes, unwise choices, he had to remedy. If Jared could do it, so could he.

Time to begin.

After hanging the calendar back on the wall, he grabbed a pair of shears and went outside to the backyard. He had no idea what his mother's favorite flower was. All he knew was she'd loved sitting at the picnic table back there, surrounded by family. A mum bouquet, from her backyard, would be his offering.

The Roanoke cemetery was ten miles and one left turn from Solitaire Farm. It would have been so easy to keep going straight, head to town and buy a gallon of milk instead of facing the past.

A handful of vehicles were in the cemetery's parking lot. One in particular caught Joel's attention: Beth's mother's car, a white four-door sedan. Joel parked a respectful distance from it and wished he'd taken the time to ask someone how he'd go about finding his parents' graves. It had occurred to him on the way over that perhaps he should have brought two bunches of flowers, but his dad, Ray McCreedy, hadn't been much for sentimental things.

Well, his dad had liked one sentimental thing: Joel's mother.

The flowers already looked a little wilted, as if

they also preferred to be back at Solitaire Farm, bending to the early-November wind instead of at this almost deserted cemetery, where the only ones intended to receive their beauty couldn't appreciate anything.

Walking up the main path, Joel tried to remember where he'd stood that long-ago day they'd buried his mother. He'd just turned eighteen, angry, hurting and feeling like he didn't belong anywhere. If he remembered, it had taken everything he had to keep from crying. If someone had even touched him that day, he'd have fallen to his knees and maybe never had the strength to stand on his own again.

Finally he saw something that looked familiar: a fountain, not working then and not working now, but with a bench right next to it. He remembered Billy sitting there, crying.

Billy had been able to cry.

Billy had also stopped crying and gone to stand with the two boys who weren't really his sons but who he loved as if they were. That long-ago day, Billy had stood by Jared and his young wife and brand new baby.

Billy, standing to Joel's left, had reached out to take Ryan, only a week old, so that Mandy could hold Jared up.

No one had held Joel up.

That day, some eight years ago, Joel had felt so alone. He'd felt like Job, after all that had been taken from him. Job had despised his life and felt it had no meaning.

So had Joel.

No one was holding him up today, either, which is why his steps faltered when he came to his mother's marker.

Eight years.

Dropping to his knees, he pulled grass from the marble headstone and laid the flowers underneath. She'd been just forty-five when she died. Not old at all. His father had been the same age at the time of his death.

Almost against his will, Joel went to stand by a newer grave.

Mandy's.

She'd been all of twenty-five. Joel remembered how she'd gone to summer school, night school and even taken online classes to graduate early. Her parents wouldn't give permission for her to marry Jared unless she finished high school.

As the November wind chilled the cemetery and sent leaves chasing the mourners home, Joel walked around, looking at names: grandparents, an uncle who died in Vietnam and next to Mandy another marker—one that caused Joel to stumble.

Maxwell Joel McCreedy.

The date of birth and the date of death were the same. Little Max, whose middle name was Joel's first, had lived but a day.

Son of Jared and Mandy.

Until We See You Again was chiseled on the marker, right underneath the engraving of a cradle.

This time when Joel hit his knees, next to a nephew he'd not even realized he had had, it wasn't to clear the grass away but to pray.

His moment of repentance was cut short by a brisk "Joel. Joel."

The last person he wanted to see, Patsy Armstrong, stood less than a respectful distance away. She looked ready to jump out of her skin, and for once he didn't think he was to blame.

"My car won't start."

"This is not a good time—" Joel began.

"Beth just called. Susan's having her baby. I have to get to the hospital."

Looked like he was needed. "Let's go," he said. "We'll worry about your car later." She beat him to his truck, didn't seem to expect it to be locked and climbed in the passenger side without waiting for his help.

Then, white-faced, she stared forward, without talking, as he backed out of the parking lot and headed for the hospital.

Maybe she was afraid of what she might say. "Thank you" would hurt. He was already breaking the speed limit. And it wasn't quite the time to say, "Stay away from my daughter."

Three police cars, all that Roanoke had, were in the parking lot. Scurrying up the sidewalk was

Linda, whose beauty salon was just a block from the hospital. She arrived at the hospital entrance at the same time that Beth opened the door and as Joel stopped the truck to deposit Patsy.

Linda opened her mouth, wisely shut it and then narrowed her eyes when Patsy said, "You don't need to escort me in."

Before he even took his foot off the brake, Beth appeared at the entrance, grabbed hold of her sister and mother and dragged them through the doors. She looked back to say, "Joel! I'm so glad you're here. Hurry up, park, meet us inside." He'd stay a minute, make Beth happy and help welcome Victoria Ann Farraday into the world.

But first, he had to park.

When he got to the waiting room, Beth and Linda were pacing while a cop, a guy Joel had gone to school with, offered advice and yet another cop said, "We've gotta go. Call if something happens."

"Mom got to go in and I didn't," Beth complained.

"I've never seen Mom so excited," Linda added.

Joel settled down next to Beth. "How on earth," she asked, "did you wind up bringing my mother to the hospital?"

"I was putting flowers on my mother's grave. She was at the cemetery and her car wouldn't start. I think I was the closest person."

"If you hadn't been there," Linda said, "she'd have had to steal a lawn mower or something. No way would she miss this."

Later, watching Beth's face when she saw her new niece through the glass partition, Joel knew he didn't want to miss this or any other of Beth's special events.

He wanted this. Even more than he wanted to rodeo, he wanted this.

It was almost seven by the time Beth convinced her mother to give Alex and Susan some time alone with their new baby. If anything, Susan would probably fall asleep the minute everyone left—half the town and most of their church family had stopped by.

Joel had been part of the family. He'd fetched an extra chair for Susan's room. He'd gone out and brought back fast food and Mom had been forced—thanks to his chauffeuring her to her granddaughter's birth—to be civil.

Joel finally ushered Beth and Patsy from the hospital and into his truck. Patsy was stuck by the passenger-side window of Joel's truck while Beth willingly took the middle. The only pall over Patsy's day was the knowledge that as soon as Joel dropped her off, Beth would be alone with him.

"You have school tomorrow," she reminded Beth when Beth walked her to the front door to make sure she got in okay.

"I know."

The house keys shook in Mom's hand as she tried to open the door. "Beth, I want you to think hard. You just watched your sister give birth. You just saw

what a happy family should look like. Yet, every time
your brother-in-law goes to work, Susan worries that
he won't come home."

"Every profession has risks, Mom."

"Not like what policemen face. At least they're
giving to the community. They're heroes. That Mc-
Creedy boy courts danger every time he gets on a
bull because he thinks it's fun."

Beth took the keys from her mother's hand and
opened the door. Mom really wasn't talking about
Joel. She was talking about her own husband.

"Mom, it's going to be okay. You should hear Joel
talking about what changes he can make at the farm.
He's planning on expanding Solitaire's Market. He
wants to—"

"He's a thief, too. He took all that money."

"Mom, we don't know that."

"We do. He took twelve thousand, three hundred
and seventy-four dollars, all earmarked for the Rodeo
Club."

Beth stepped back. "Bye, Mom. I really have to
go. I'm tired, and Joel's waiting."

He'd left the engine running and a slow song was
playing on the country radio station. Joel leaned
back, eyes closed.

"It's been a long day," Beth said after she climbed
in beside him, scooting over to take the middle part
of the seat.

"You have no idea," Joel said, as he drove off.

"I'm glad you went to the cemetery. I meant to tell

you earlier, but every time I turned around somebody new was in the room and I couldn't seem to get you alone."

"Do you remember Caleb's birthday party?"

"I remember watching you help put up the inflatable house. I remember you taking Matt aside and helping him feel comfortable in a crowd."

"Do you remember what you said to me?"

Unfortunately, Beth did. "I said you'd be gone by Thanksgiving."

Joel laughed, but it wasn't exactly a sound of joy. "I'd forgotten that. Thanksgiving's in just a few weeks. Do you still think I'm leaving?"

"No."

Joel turned off the radio and pulled into Beth's driveway. She snuggled up next to him, worried about him, and wanting to touch him, comfort him. "Joel, what is it?"

"I put flowers on my mother's grave. I cleaned off my dad's, my grandparents' and Mandy's."

"Oh."

"*Oh* is right. I found Maxwell Joel McCreedy's grave. You want to tell me about it before I ask Jared?"

"Where is Jared?"

"He took the kids to see Mandy's parents. They'll be back late tonight."

"They've been begging him to come." Beth stared out the front windshield, at the little house she shared with her sister. It had a postage-stamp lawn and the porch only big enough for two.

It was no longer enough for Beth. She wanted a bigger place, with a lawn that Joel mowed, and half a dozen children raking the leaves and making a mess that Joel would grumble about and clean up.

Like Jared used to do with the three boys while Mandy laughed and made a mess with the kids.

"Mandy said that Jared hit the roof when she chose Max's name with yours as the middle. But, there she was, already sick while pregnant with Caleb and Max, and then Max didn't make it."

"How? Why did he not make it?"

"They listed it as a congenital anomaly. Mandy'd already started treatment for the cancer when she found out she was pregnant. She stopped immediately. They couldn't say for sure why Max didn't make it, no more than they could say why Caleb did."

Beth felt her throat closing. Joel reached over and brushed away an errant tear before taking her hand and entwining his fingers in hers. "By the time she got out of the hospital, Max was already buried. Mandy claimed that Jared decided what to inscribe, but Jared denied it. I never knew who to believe."

It took a few minutes for Joel to share everything he'd experienced that morning, but he did it in such a way that Beth felt she was right there with him even up to the moment her mother interrupted him. It was a type of sharing she'd never felt before. She saw his passion, his vulnerability and his acceptance.

She felt as if she were a part of him.

Did he feel it, too?

"I'm not going away again," Joel said, "not like I did the first time. I was running away. I thought that the only way I could be happy was if I just had myself to worry about. I don't think I've really been happy since."

"Not even when you won?"

"Without family cheering you on, it's a hollow victory."

"Family is not always easy," Beth said. The words sounded stilted. If Joel had felt left out by what happened to his family, Beth had felt suffocated by what had happened to hers. Her mother wanted to control her daughters like a master puppeteer.

"Joel," Beth said softly, "about my mother."

"I'll change her mind. She'll see what a great guy I can be."

"She doesn't know you, not like I do."

"If it's between bull riding and you," Joel said, "I pick you. Would that be enough? Would that convince your mother?"

"I honestly don't know," Beth said. "And I don't want you to quit. I think it's exciting and I want to come to the rodeos and cheer."

Joel gently turned Beth's head so she faced him. Then, with one finger, he tilted her head so he could lean down and kiss her. Gently, slowly, deeply. A kiss that promised forever.

"We'll change your mother's mind," he promised, his voice husky.

Beth tried to catch her breath. She didn't want

to say anything to change the mood, but she also wanted to find a way to make things right. "Mom keeps going back to the missing RC money. She can't seem to forget you're accused of stealing twelve thousand, three hundred and seventy-four dollars."

"And she thinks she saw me in the hallway that night. She even told the police."

"And the reporter."

Joel almost chuckled. "We're making it worse."

"Before we make it better."

"I'll find out who took the money," Joel promised.

"We'll find out," Beth corrected him. "I can ask around. Working at the school means I can get hold of records."

Joel thought back to the only lead he really had. Billy claimed they'd never gotten around to counting the RC money. Frank Peabody agreed, pointing to the minutes and treasury reports he'd kept. Yet, someone had given both Beth's mother and Jared a specific amount.

Chapter Eighteen

It was almost nine when Joel got home. Solitaire Farm remained silent, waiting for family to turn it from an empty dwelling to a bustling home. Joel turned on the lights and wished the ghosts of his past didn't hover quite so close. He could still see his father sitting in the green La-Z-Boy, falling asleep during the early news. He could hear his mother in the kitchen, singing while she cleaned up after supper. He could envision Mandy and her friends sewing in the living room.

He could smell Beth's perfume and feel the warmth of her as she stood next to him at the kitchen counter handing him crackers to add to the meat loaf.

Joel wanted to smile, but somehow the memories—whether old or new—felt fleeting.

After making a pot of coffee, never mind how late it was, Joel took the three folders Frank Peabody had given him on Saturday and spread them on the table.

Then, he pulled his cell phone from his back pocket and called the man.

"Hope it's not too late."

"Just watching the news."

"I have a few facts," Joel said. "I want to double-check. My stepfather says there was no opportunity to count the money. Your daughter's minutes say the same thing. You yourself mentioned that you'd planned to meet up with Billy in the morning to count everything, but the money went missing before you could. Yet, you have an amount written down. How did you arrive at that number?"

"I recorded what Jared paid us."

"He's not here right now. Do you remember him saying anything to you about who told him the amount?"

"Except for recording and depositing his check, I never dealt with Jared. That would have been your stepfather or the Rodeo Club president, I'm guessing."

"Who was the RC president?"

Mr. Peabody chuckled. "My daughter Meg."

"Would you call her and ask her how she got that number?"

"Right away."

Joel heard the sounds of his brother's minivan before he finished his first cup of coffee.

Jared carried Caleb in and then went back out for

Matt. Ryan dragged in under his own steam and went right to bed.

"Who knew Veteran's Day could be so much fun? We had a great time. They'll survive one night without a bath," Jared said, walking up the stairs. "If it's really bad, they can take one before school."

Joel stuck a bag of popcorn in the microwave and waited for Jared to come back down the stairs. When Jared finally did, it was after a long shower and the popcorn would have been cold if Joel had waited.

Jared went and heated his own bag, ignored Joel's coffee, poured himself a glass of milk and then sat at the table, fingering the papers Joel had spread out. "This doesn't look like the makings of a rope-and-pulley bull."

"These are the treasury reports that Mr. Peabody dropped off on Saturday afternoon. During physical therapy, he and I talk. I keep telling everyone that I didn't take the RC money and thought maybe I could prove it."

"Okay," Jared said slowly.

"Mr. Peabody was treasurer back then. He remembers quite a bit."

"Like?"

"Do you remember Billy saying that they never counted the money?"

"Yes."

"Mr. Peabody says the same thing."

"Okay," Jared said.

"You paid an exact amount. That first night I was home you whipped the number out as if it were tattooed on your brain."

"Twelve thousand, three hundred and seventy-four dollars."

"Where did you get the amount? Because Peabody says all he did was record what you paid him."

"I always thought it was Billy."

The phone rang. Joel snatched it up, not wanting the boys to awaken. Instead of Mr. Peabody, he got Meg.

"Dad says you're asking more questions. I have no idea why Jared paid the amount he did. I just know that everyone kept saying that we'd made twice what we'd made the year before."

"Check the report from nine years ago," Joel told Jared. "How much did the RC make?"

It took Jared but a moment to find the right spreadsheet and then the exact listing he wanted. "Four thousand, eight hundred and fifteen."

Joel shared the number with Meg.

"Quite a difference. If you times that by two, you get just under ten thousand dollars," she said. "What does your brother say?"

"He says he thought Billy told him how much, but Billy says no."

"I've always just had it in my mind that Billy gave the amount," Meg said.

"Thanks, Meg," Joel said. "I appreciate the quick call back." He hung up the phone, sat down, took a long drink of cold coffee and tried to convince himself that the eerie feeling in his bones was fatigue. He didn't want to be right, didn't want to be thinking what he was thinking. Yet his gut said otherwise. Turning to his brother, he said, "Tonight somebody else repeated to me that amount you repaid."

Jared's eyes widened. "Who?"

"Beth."

"Beth didn't take that money. She would have been all of fourteen and scared of her mother."

"I think maybe Beth was quoting her mother."

The next morning rolled around much too quickly. Joel woke before the alarm. After starting the pancakes for the whole crowd, he called Nathan Fisher and rescheduled his session for later that afternoon.

While Jared doled out the pancakes, Joel added syrup: a lot for Caleb, just right for Ryan and hardly any for Matt.

"Where are you going this morning instead of therapy?" Jared asked. After last night's talk, his big brother wanted to be involved, too. And, like Joel, he hoped they were wrong about Patsy Armstrong.

"Little pitchers have big ears," Joel said.

Instead of shoveling down his food and heading for the field like he usually did, Jared ate leisurely. Once the boys headed upstairs to dress for school, he repeated his question.

"I'm heading to Freeport."

"Why?"

"The day Peabody dropped the minutes and treasury reports off, he mentioned that it wasn't the first time Beth's mom had helped solve a crime and save the school some money. You know she's the one who claimed to have seen me in the hallway."

"I remember. What else has she done?"

"About two years ago, according to Frank Peabody, there was a rash of computer stuff going missing. Portable devices like laptops, new jump drives, things that would be easy to resell and make a quick profit. All in all, in a five-year period, the school lost over ten thousand in reported theft. Mrs. Armstrong finally interrupted a break-in, caught a couple boys and the crimes stopped."

"And you're thinking?"

"I don't know what I'm thinking, but I found the newspaper articles and asked Alex to find the police report. The kids live just an hour drive away. I want to go talk to them."

"Have you called to make sure they still live there or even that they're willing to talk to you?"

"They both have local addresses, and I don't want to take a chance they'll say no. I think once they see me, hear me out, they'll be more willing to talk."

"I'll come with you," Jared offered.

"Why?"

If Joel had been surprised by the offer, he was even more surprised by the reasoning behind it. "Because I'm your brother and it's time we cleared your name."

He didn't mention the money at all.

* * *

November, for most of Iowa, meant downtime. Harvest was pretty much over, and farmers were thinking about crop rotation and next year's seed. Freeport looked like a town ready for snow.

"It's due," Jared said after Joel mentioned it. "We usually have a couple of inches in October. Last few years, the weather's been crazy."

"For the rodeo, too," Joel said. "In the last year, I've sometimes felt like I've gone to more dances than events. If there's even a hint that the arena is unsafe, they cancel. We get our entry fee back but that's like getting your letter back from Santa Claus and no toy."

"You've been hanging around my sons too much."

"And enjoying every minute. What was the address again?"

"Jerry Tate lives on Cypress Street. According to the map, it's about midway through town and behind city hall."

It took Joel a few minutes to find city hall. Then, he turned down a street boasting middle-class, white clapboard homes with a family feel.

Jared said, "You plan to tell Beth what you're doing?"

"No, because I hope I'm wrong."

"I don't think you are. All these years I've never questioned your guilt, and I should have. It occurs to me that besides Billy, the one person who I'd listen to concerning the amount would be Patsy. She always acted more like a vice principal than a secretary. Billy often complained about having to rein her in."

"And all I can think," Joel complained, "is that I'm trying to take down the one woman I need to win over."

They parked the minivan in the street. It looked right at home. There were probably five or more minivans interspersed between the few trucks and sedans that hadn't delivered their owners to work or other locations. Joel went to the front door and knocked. Jared was right behind him.

The woman who opened the door reminded Joel of Beth's big sister Linda. She was perfectly dressed, as if just about ready to go out, and if the sight of two overgrown cowboys at her door spooked her, she didn't show it. "May I help you?"

"We're looking for Jerry Tate."

She won more brownie points when she didn't ask, "What's he done?" or "Are you the police?"

"Why are you looking for Jerry?"

"My name's Joel McCreedy. I live in Roanoke—"

Her face twitched slightly, not a good sign, so Joel hurried on before she decided to stop being neighborly.

"—and about eight years ago, I had some trouble at Roanoke Elementary. I'm trying to clear my name. I was hoping your brother might have some ideas that could help."

"Stay right here." She closed the door and locked it.

Joel looked at Jared. "I'm feeling hopeful."

"I'd feel more hopeful if she had invited us in."

"We're strangers and we're asking questions about something that must be a bad memory. She's doing the right thing."

It was a good five minutes before the door opened again. The woman held a portable phone and was talking into it. "Yes, tell him Joel McCreedy the cowboy is in our living room right now. Give him his lunch break early if you have to." There was a long pause. "No, you don't have to come home, but if you want to, come ahead. It might be interesting."

Then, she hung up and stepped out of the way. "Jerry works with his dad at Binky's Hamburgers. They're doing prep for lunch and can probably come home for thirty minutes or so."

Jared found his manners first. "And you are?"

"Cathy Tate." The frown she aimed at Joel wasn't real. "Jerry's mother, not his sister." The living room they entered was clean but cluttered. Books were piled five high on end tables. One-fourth of the room was devoted to Legos. A flat screen television dominated the room.

Joel and Jared sat on a couch that felt much too small. Cathy Tate went into the kitchen and came out with two bottled waters. "I did a Google search on you, but even before that I thought I recognized you. Jerry talked about being a bull rider for a while. One of his friends is starting the circuit now that they've graduated. You're a name he brings up as a local even though you're in the next town over. First time Jerry flew through the air, his desire to do it a second time flew out the window."

Any other day, Joel would have felt ridiculously pleased at being recognized for his bull riding skills. Today, he was just glad the recognition got him through the front door.

"I didn't," Cathy continued, "find anything that referenced a crime in Roanoke, although I found that your family has a farm there."

"I wasn't charged."

Jared spoke up. "I'm his big brother. You didn't find a reference because I reimbursed the school before it got that far. Now I'm wishing I hadn't because my brother didn't take the money."

"After all this time you suddenly believe him?" Cathy asked.

"After all this time," Jared said, "I'm taking the time to listen to him."

"Well, we listened to Jerry, too. And he did break into the school and he did try to steal the laptops. I'm not sure we can help. What exactly are you trying to prove?"

"That somebody's been taking big money from Roanoke Elementary for years and managing to pass the blame to others." Until he said the words, Joel hadn't quite believed it himself, but everything he discovered pointed to such a scenario.

"Well, if that's what you're looking for, you might be in luck."

The sound of a car pulling into the driveway stopped her. She got up and went to the door, opening it to usher in a balding man about ten years older than Jared and a lanky kid with a too-young face still peppered by acne and a goatee that any self-respecting goat would laugh at.

Joel stood, walked over to Jerry and said, "Thank you so much for taking off work to talk with me. I think we have something in common."

Jerry glanced at his dad before answering, "What?"

Joel and Jared explained. Jerry nodded. "Dad, I'll meet you back at work—this won't take long." Jerry and his mother led Joel and Jared to the kid's bedroom. It was as cluttered as the living room, only Jerry preferred DVDs and empty plates plus lots of clothes on the floor.

"I didn't have a decent computer two years ago," he explained. "And I knew that as long as my old one still worked, I wouldn't get a new one unless I did something."

Joel perched on the edge of the bed. Jerry's mother sat next to him. Jared stayed in the doorway.

A few clicks on the computer and a site came up that advertised all kinds of items, from clothes to DVDs to computers. "I kept checking this site to see if I could find a new or used laptop cheap enough, but the ones I could afford were worse than the one I had. One day, I was looking at this really cool laptop and down below, where the comments were, was an entry about how easy it was to steal laptops from elementary schools.

"I was stupid," Jerry admitted. "But I read the comment, thought it sounded easy and convinced my best buddy to go with me. Honestly, until we were in the school and really doing it, it all felt like a dream."

"More like a nightmare," his mother said. "I wanted to blame his best buddy. Instead, the other mother got to blame my kid."

"Try to remember exactly what the comment said," Joel urged.

"It talked about the number of kids purposely leaving windows unlocked so they could come back late at night and steal."

"And that's what my kid did," said Cathy. "He drove to Roanoke and found an open window at the school. He and Greg had five laptops in their possession when that teacher caught them."

Joel didn't correct her about Mrs. Armstrong's job title. "Show me the comment," he directed Jerry.

"That's the thing," Jerry said. "The police wanted to see the comment, too, but when I went back to the site, the laptop had been sold and the entire page deleted."

"I don't think you can ever completely delete anything," Joel mused.

"Well, the cops didn't try much to find it because it didn't matter, not for my case, anyway. Mom took away my computer privileges, so I didn't get to look for it again for quite a while."

"Without that comment, you'd never have tried to steal a laptop."

Jerry looked at his mom. "I don't know. I do know that I wouldn't have tried it right then."

"What made you pick Roanoke?" Jared asked, still standing in the doorway.

"The comment listed ten schools that were easy targets. Roanoke was the closest."

As Jerry's mom ushered them out the front door, she asked, "Do you think my boy was lured there?"

"I'll let you know the minute I find out," Joel promised.

Back in the minivan, Jared got behind the wheel and asked, "We going to look up this Greg kid?"

"No, I found out more than I expected from this one." As Jared pointed the vehicle back home, Joel took out his cell phone and tapped in the number Billy had provided once he trusted that his stepsons and grandchildren wouldn't come and kidnap him and make him stay home.

He answered on the second ring. Joel had one question. "How good is Patsy on a computer, especially on the internet?"

Billy's response was immediate. "We didn't have to hire an outsider to do the school's website. Patsy did it. When we purchased the grade software, she headed the committee."

"That good?"

"I used to say if we lost her, Bill Gates needed to find her. Why?"

"I'll tell you more when I find out more." Joel shut off the phone and put it in his pocket.

"So," Jared said, "what are you going to do with this information?"

Joel stared out the window, realizing he was talking to the only other person who might ever know the truth. "When we headed for Freeport this morning, I was worried about what we'd find and how it would affect my chances with Beth."

"And now?"

"I'm beyond worry. If I tell the authorities, then I'm the one who pointed the finger at the mother of the woman I love."

"And if you don't tell," Jared said, "you'll forever be known as the McCreedy boy who stole the Rodeo Club money."

"I lose either way."

Chapter Nineteen

Was it Beth's imagination or was Joel's greeting a little stilted? "I looked for you this morning," she said. "I had recess duty and was hoping for a little company."

"Jared and I had some business in Freeport. We left right after dropping the boys off."

"You take Caleb with you?" She motioned to the small boy sound asleep in Joel's arms.

"He spent part of the morning in day care. I think that's why he's so tired."

She waited, noticing how distracted he was and trying not to question too much. All she knew was that at the moment, this was not the same man she'd been with all of yesterday.

"When I'm finished here, I'm heading for the hospital to see my niece. If you and the boys stick around, I'll treat us at the Ice Cream Shack after."

Ryan and Matt thought that was a great idea.

"We can even do homework there," Beth offered, "and I'll help."

There was a sadness in his eyes that hadn't been there yesterday. Something had changed. Beth fought the urge to snap her fingers and demand he tell her what was wrong. Just yesterday, he couldn't get enough of her. And this was one time when her mother couldn't be blamed. Patsy was at the hospital with her granddaughter. First time she'd missed a workday in all of Beth's memory. No, it was doubtful Mom could be blamed for Joel's strange mood.

"Joel, are you all right? Did something happen in Freeport?"

"I need to get the boys home," he said, avoiding her questions. "It's been a tough day. I'll tell you about Freeport some other time."

"Is there anything I can do?"

Joel shook his head, effortlessly changing Caleb from his right side to his left. "No, everything's in my court now. Fisher gave me a release form. I've already downloaded the paperwork I need for the November Mesquite Rodeo."

It felt like the sidewalk had disappeared under Beth, and she couldn't think of anything to say. Joel didn't seem to notice. He walked across the parking lot to the minivan, Caleb in his arms and the two boys following right behind, with Ryan doing all the talking. People stopped to talk to him, pat him on the back. He'd only been home almost two months and already he was a fixture, to the town and to her.

That he would leave for the Mesquite Holiday Rodeo didn't surprise her. He'd already mentioned it; she'd expected it, but she had somehow believed that when he left, he'd ask her to go with him.

Today, he hadn't issued an invite.

Maybe his bad mood had to do with making choices?

Looking around the school yard, she realized that their little corner of the world went on. The safety patrol kids were still walking students to cars. The principal still called out names using the megaphone that was much too loud. The third grade teacher, brand new this year, furtively engaged in text messaging when she should be watching her students, and as for Beth, she looked to see who she had left.

Three kindergartners—thanks to her inattention— had their lunch boxes open and were sharing leftover food.

This one time, Beth didn't care.

Finally, their parents came and Beth headed for her classroom. The only good thing she could think of was that her mother wasn't here to witness Beth's mood. Mom was at the hospital making sure her granddaughter was safe.

Safe.

Such an important word to Patsy Armstrong.

Right now, to Beth's way of thinking, feeling loved

was more important than feeling safe. But that was silly feminine angst, and Beth was better than that. Truly, Joel might just be having an off day.

She hurriedly tidied up her classroom and prepped for the next day. Matt's work had turned around. He was doing everything she asked and doing it well. She could only hope the improvements continued even after Joel left.

Today, Roanoke Hospital didn't boast three police cars in its parking lot. Either her brother-in-law had gone to work or he was out fetching bubblegum ice cream and blueberry topping. Beth parked her Chevy a good distance from the front doors and walked inside. She'd been allowed to hold little Victoria only once yesterday, and this evening she meant to spend a little more quality time with her new niece.

Walking into her sister's room, she was glad to see that the only other visitor was Linda.

"Where's Mom?"

"One of her friends came to see the baby and the two of them are downstairs getting something to eat. You should have seen me." Linda flexed a muscle. "I had to physically escort them out."

"Mom's driving me crazy," Susan said drowsily. "Every time I start to fall asleep, she makes a suggestion. It was dark when she left last night and dark when she showed up this morning."

Beth wanted to say that Mom was excited, but she wasn't feeling too kindly toward Mom right now. In her heart of hearts, she still harbored fear that Patsy Armstrong had something to do with Joel's attitude today.

"Come on, sis," Linda said. "Let's walk down to the nursery so you can see how much Vicky has grown."

"Victoria," Susan corrected.

"We've got to get Mom home," Linda said the moment they got out of the room. "Susan's about to have a nervous breakdown, and I think Alex's gone back to work just so he can research legitimate reasons to arrest an overzealous new grandmother. And," she added, "I'm just glad Susan's doing this first so that when you and I have babies, Mom will have to divide her time."

"If we ever have babies." Beth looked through the hospital glass at the three infants in their tight blankets and thin, pointy knitted hats. Victoria, the only girl, was in the middle. She was sleeping peacefully, unaware that in twenty years one or both of the boys flanking her might cause her to paint her toenails a funky green or even make her think of defying her mother and following the rodeo.

"Okay, sis, spill. You're not standing there with tears in your eyes because you're so enraptured with Vicky."

"Victoria," Beth corrected.

"What did Joel do?"

"Nothing. He picked the boys up from school, said he'd had a tough day and didn't mention yesterday."

"What happened yesterday besides Victoria making her appearance and Mom having him chauffeur her here?"

"He kissed me."

"Umm."

"No, he *really* kissed me."

"And mentally you started picking out wedding dresses."

Beth started to deny it but shrugged instead. Linda was her roommate. She knew that Beth had started thinking *wedding dress* from the time Joel called her that Saturday to help with Solitaire's Market and Matt.

Linda willingly gave advice. "You have to ignore him. He's a cowboy. He does the chasing or there's no victory."

"He's a cowboy, all right," Beth muttered. "On top of everything else, he's just gotten his medical release and can enter rodeos again."

"That's great," Linda said.

As if in sympathy, Victoria opened her mouth and squalled. The boys on either side startled. Then they, too, began to scream.

"Now," Linda continued, "you'll never have to wonder if he settled. He'll either choose you, choose the rodeo or choose both. You have a two out of three chance of getting the cowboy of your dreams."

"Too bad the cowboy of my dreams is my mother's nightmare."

"Yeah, well, Mom married the man of her dreams

more than thirty years ago, and it's time she remembered just how that made her feel instead of only remembering how losing him made her feel."

In the nursery, the nurse had slipped a binky in Victoria's mouth and already, looking both innocent and content, the baby had fallen back to sleep.

If only Beth's fears could be so easily eliminated.

"What are you going to do?" Jared asked, coming from the kitchen after checking on Ryan and Matt and their homework. He'd had to tell Ryan for the third time to turn off his Game Boy. This time, Jared had taken the game and was actually playing it as he walked into the living room.

Unlike Joel, Jared no longer needed to look at the notes and calendar Billy had left him. Had and the boys had made their own routines.

When Joel didn't answer, Jared added, "Short term, we're going to church. We need to leave in about twenty minutes. Long term, what are you going to do?"

"I don't have to decide right away. I'm going to do a few rodeos. There's one in Texas I'm interested in. If I leave right after the Fall Festival, I'll just make it. I want to see what happens both there, and then…"

"You're running away again."

"It's not that easy. Every time I think about what to do, I imagine the repercussions."

"Every time you've gotten on the bull, have you imagined the repercussions?"

"Absolutely."

"But you still get back on," Jared pointed out.

"I'm not in the love with the bull."

Jared put the hard plastic Game Boy on the coffee table next to all the papers Joel had spread out. He went to one of the end tables that flanked the green couch and pulled out a worn book that Joel easily recognized.

Unlike the fairly new Game Boy, their father's aged Bible had survived decades of use in the Mc-Creedy household. The gold engraving on the front was so worn that the word *Bible* had completely disappeared. Some of the pages were torn and sticking out from the book at odd angles. A stain, possibly coffee, darkened one corner.

"I found it the day Billy left," Jared said. "I'm not sure if it had always been in that little drawer or whether Billy put it there on purpose."

He folded his hands in front of him and shook his head. "For six months, I hated this house, hated this kitchen and hated my life."

"I'm so—"

Jared held up his hand. "When I thought things couldn't get worse, you came back. I truly thought God hated me. I mean, I'd always gone to church, read the Bible, did what was right and none of that helped keep Mandy alive."

Joel didn't move. He was afraid to. One wrong move, and the grip he had on his emotions might shatter.

"I thought about running away," Jared said. "No one cared what I was doing. The boys are too young to appreciate the hard work I do every day keeping this a working farm. Billy went from here to school to his committee meetings to church with no time to stop and dwell about all he'd lost. Me, I had plenty of time while riding the combine, all alone in the cab with only a field of corn to keep me company."

Jared wasn't done. "I'd watch the teeth on the gathering chain as it separated the corn ears from the corn plants. And I felt like this place was swallowing me whole. I knew that behind me, the cobs and husks were being spit out. I wished I could release my anger the same way, but I couldn't. Like you, I wanted to run away, but there was a difference."

"What?"

"I didn't know where to go."

Joel didn't have a response. He'd been young and foolish when he had headed for the rodeo. He'd felt invincible. Plus, he hadn't had three sons who needed caring for.

"Because I stayed," Jared said, "I finally found out that I'm one of the luckiest men in the world."

Not what Joel had been expecting.

Jared picked up the Bible. "All that time I wasn't

alone in the cab. God was there. He answered the prayers I didn't have the strength to ask."

"Dad!" It was Matt's voice in a panic. "I can't find my homework!"

"Two months ago, he'd have shouted Billy's name. A week ago, he'd have called for you. Today, he wants me." Jared stood, leaving the Bible on the coffee table, right on top of Billy's calendar.

Matt called for his dad again, but Jared didn't leave. Instead, he said, "Nowhere in the Bible does it talk of someone being victorious by walking away from right."

Joel didn't have a comeback.

"If it's bothering you this much, I can go in your place," Jared offered.

"No, I need to talk to Beth."

Finally, Jared turned toward the kitchen, but not before stating, "What you need to do is talk to her mother."

And, no doubt, both would be at the Fall Festival committee meeting tonight.

Joel looked at Billy's calendar, which now felt more like his own. The festival was just five days away. Tonight was the last meeting, where the details would be hammered out and, hopefully, all problems solved. In that area, things were looking good. The mechanical bulls both worked, and Joel had plenty of volunteers to help with concessions.

There was an hour before Joel needed to leave for the final committee meeting. Jared and the boys didn't need him. He felt the urge to pace, move, escape, but Joel remained where he was—looking at his father's Bible.

Finally, Joel reached for it. There wasn't much he could find about running away, so finally he settled on the first book of Corinthians, the ninth chapter.

"Do you not know that in a race all the runners run, but only one gets the prize?"

For a moment, Joel considered the prize to be winning the National Championship. The rodeo he wouldn't be participating in because of his injury, not this year, or next. Probably ever.

"Run in such a way as to get the prize."

Joel could handle that.

"Everyone who competes in the games goes into strict training. They do it to get a crown that will not last..."

Not what Joel wanted to see next, think about next. But, in some ways, it was a wake-up call.

Swallowing, Joel tried to remind himself what rodeo prize he was after: a buckle, a purse, a sponsorship.

Unfortunately, Beth Armstrong was the only prize he wanted.

Joel took a seat in the sixth grade classroom hosting the final committee meeting and stared at Patsy Armstrong.

Usually she came across as a person with a mission. Tonight was the same, but instead of settling in and tapping on a desktop to garner attention, she waited patiently—looking more tense than in charge—while Max went over a few things with Meg Peabody.

Once Beth entered the room, Meg kept giving Joel looks. She wasn't the only one. It didn't take a rocket scientist to realize that the investigation Joel had instigated might go on with or without him. This day, Mona didn't suggest Beth sit with Joel. Instead, Mona patted Beth on the shoulder and gave Beth's mother a disapproving look.

Not what Joel wanted.

Not what God wanted.

Finally, Meg straightened, passed out an agenda sheet and sat down to take notes.

Max took charge, emphasizing set-up schedules, insurance concerns and expectations.

"The best news," Joel started with, "has to do with the bulls. Max tried them last night. Both work great. And members of the volunteer fire department—all with medical training—have volunteered to operate the two bulls."

"Perfect," said Max. "Trey's been talking about this all week."

"I'm not finished," Joel continued. "Billy called tonight. He'll be back Monday. Tomorrow. He's all set to assist with concessions."

"Do you still need Patsy?" Max asked.

Her face went a little pale. Her strained expression tightened. For a moment, Joel thought she might not answer, but instead she said, "Billy didn't stop money from going missing last time."

It was all Joel could do to sit on his hands and not say, "Yeah, right into your pocket."

"Mother," Beth hissed, shooting Joel an apologetic look.

Joel had to give her credit. Beth seemed to know something was bothering him and was willing to give him space. There were no forgotten backpacks, no chance meetings and absolutely no fun at all involved in school pick-up and drop-off times.

"Patsy," Joel said. "I look forward to working with you. I think you have a lot to teach me about keeping track of money."

Chapter Twenty

Come Monday, Beth could only watch as Joel threw himself into the preparation of the Fall Festival with impressive fervor, so much so that when he walked Matt to class, he absentmindedly said, "Be good," more to Beth than to Matt.

She'd been good for twenty-two years! She didn't need him to make the suggestion. She needed him to make a better one.

Be mine, instead of *be good.*

All day, she was aware that Joel was just a few yards away, painting backdrops, running electrical cords and constructing booths. At three, both Joel and Billy showed up at her classroom door. Matt practically knocked his desk over he was so excited.

On Wednesday, they passed in the school hallway. Beth gave a nod in greeting; Joel did exactly the same.

That's not what happened when Joel and her mother almost bumped into each other that evening at church. They both came to a full stop; neither acted like they intended to be the one to give the right-of-way.

Since Joel's return, he and her mother had played bumper cars with each other, giving as good as they received. But since the last committee meeting, and even though it was obvious to everyone that Beth and Joel's interest in each other had hit a rough spot, her mother seemed more underhanded in her gibes. Before, Beth always knew exactly what button Mom was trying to push with Joel, be it his career choice, his lack of family commitment or his tarnished reputation thanks to the missing Rodeo Club Fund money.

Now her mother's insults were cryptic. Beth had overheard, "You don't care who you hurt." And, "Sometimes if you don't let sleeping dogs lie you get bit."

After a moment, Joel basically turned on his heel and left her mother standing in the church hallway, the words still lingering in the air. But each time Beth saw the expression on his face, she couldn't help but think that a picture was worth a thousand words.

The picture on Joel's face, every time he encountered her mother, depicted stoic acceptance as if he'd reach some sort of resolution he wasn't completely happy about.

But, about what?

Worse, Beth knew in her heart of hearts that her

mother had truly, somehow, ended any chance Beth had with Joel.

For once, her Bible didn't offer an answer she understood. Plus, Beth had never seen her mother so miserable. Even Susan had called because Mom had stopped coming by to see the baby. More than anything, Beth wanted to know why and how her mother had so much influence over Joel. Even more than that, she wanted to know what gave Joel so much power over her mother.

Every day that passed just brought more of the same. Finally, the day of the festival arrived and with it came the first snow. The students, especially Beth's kindergartners, couldn't be subdued. On top of dealing with wet boots drying by the coatrack and frozen fingers, during recess duty she overheard Ryan talking about how his uncle was leaving tonight for a distant rodeo. Matt didn't look too happy about losing his uncle.

Beth understood completely.

By the time three o'clock rolled around, Beth was ready for a hot bath, a good book and a good cry.

Still, she didn't even bother going home. It was cold and wet and she'd just have to turn around again in an hour. She had an old clown suit in her classroom closet, her acrylic paints were new and there was plenty to do before the festival officially opened at six o'clock.

Taking a breath, she headed for the gymnasium and the booth assigned to her. She didn't need much, just a comfortable chair for her and one for whoever's cheek she was painting. She had a poster all ready. The artistic choices had doubled since last year, when she first tried her hand at the art.

It only took ten minutes to prep. Then she looked around for something else to do. If it weren't for Joel's change of heart, she'd be over at the concession stand helping him stock sodas and bottles of water in coolers, helping him stack paper goods and utensils.

And hoping he'd steal a kiss when no one was looking.

What she might do, just to get his attention, was take a ride on the rope-and-pulley bull. She half expected the gymnasium floor to tilt in the direction of the bull, so many people intended to ride.

Joel, in just two months, had won over the community as well as her heart.

Her broken heart.

"Hey, guess what I have?" Linda stumbled to a halt right in front of Beth.

"A big shopping bag?"

"No." Linda grabbed Beth's arm and dragged her out of the gymnasium. Pulling her sister to the girls' restroom, she urged Beth into one of the shower stalls and opened the bag. "I found these today at a thrift store, and I knew they'd cheer you up."

From the bag, Linda pulled the perfect outfit for Beth. It was a French painter's costume, with an extra-large beret, a paint-smeared smock and a giant paintbrush that was really a squirt gun.

"Wow," Beth said, taking the costume. "Thank you. I've never seen anything so right."

"I couldn't believe they had such a perfect costume. I went home, washed it and brought it immediately over here. Anything to make you smile again. Come on, let's change. I'll be the clown."

Linda offered to share duties at the face painting booth, although her ability was more toward loud colors and abstract art. They changed—Linda giggling and Beth trying to—and then they headed for the booth, where Linda painted a tiny black mustache under Beth's nose.

Before the paint was dry, Mitzi Gabor sat down in the chair opposite Beth and said, "Can you do Cinderella?"

Two hours, fifty kids and nine Cinderellas later, Beth gave her spot over to Linda. Stretching, she looked around the crowded room. This year, thanks to the first snowfall, everyone seemed in an even more festive mood than ever. Banners celebrating one hundred years of Fall Festivals were taped on almost every wall. Each booth had a line of five or more kids.

Everyone was having a good time.

Except for Beth.

Maybe the best place to go would be her classroom. She could lock the door, pull a book from her purse and try to take her mind off of Joel.

Only one book could do that: the Bible.

Even as she turned to head for the gymnasium doors and her classroom, her stomach growled, reminding her that she'd not eaten in eight hours. She was sure a hot dog would stick in her throat and so would a hamburger. Maybe she could handle just a bowl of chili from the cook-off.

She got in line—not Joel's or her mother's—and waited her turn. Feeling incognito as they had expected her to be a clown, she got to watch her mother with her mother not realizing it. Mom's facial expression clearly read that the concession booth was not the best place for her. She could see that Joel, Jared and Billy were a team. Billy, as if he'd never been gone, worked with his stepsons with precision. Both Jared and Billy couldn't seem to stop laughing, tossing bags of chips to each other. Each time they sold a bowl of chili, they fanned themselves as if it were too hot.

Joel was doing the same but without the laughter.

Beth felt a little better when he caught sight of her. He dropped the bag of chips he was holding, but quickly regained his composure. He passed the chips, a burger and a drink to one of the Gabor parents, took the twenty they offered and handed it to Beth's mom.

Mom handed back some change.

Beth took one step forward and immediately felt her knees start to give as a small body plowed into hers.

"Matt!"

"Sorry, Miss Armstrong. I need to go to the potty." Before she could regain her footing or caution Matt about looking where he was going, someone caught her under the elbow and helped her get stabilized. She turned to thank Mr. Peabody, but lost her voice when she caught sight of her mother.

Pocketing a twenty that Joel had just passed her.

Beth's mouth dropped open. Before she could close it, as if drawn by a magnet, Mom looked over, saw Beth and recognized her.

And Beth recognized the expression on her mom's pallid face as guilt, agonizing guilt.

The loud roar of the room diminished. Beth felt for a moment like she was in a vacuum. Glancing around, she could see that no one, not even Mr. Peabody standing right behind her, had seen her mother's action. Before she could make up her mind about what to do, she looked at Joel.

Someone had seen. He looked from her to her mother.

Her mother's hand was shaking as she pulled the twenty from her pocket and put it in the cash drawer.

If that wasn't enough to make Beth's world come crashing down, what she noticed next did.

Joel didn't look surprised.

"Here!" Joel handed the bowl of chili to the man standing next in line.

"I didn't order chili."

"On the house." Joel quickly moved out from behind the counter and squeezed though the corner of the concession booth that served as their exit.

The concession area was in the middle of the gymnasium, with tables scattered around. At this peak hour, just eight o'clock, it was standing room only. Joel didn't let that stop him. He made it to the open gymnasium door, past the woman selling tickets, and into the school hallway in under eight seconds.

He wanted to be faster. This wasn't for the buckle; this was for something even more important: love.

Matt was standing in the drinking fountain line.

"You see your teacher?" Joel asked.

"She went in our classroom. I've never heard her slam the door before. We always get in trouble if we do that."

Joel sprinted the rest of the way down the hall, stopping by the heavy brown door adorned with detailed bear cutouts, announcing the names of her students.

He tried the knob.

Locked.

"Beth." He knocked, leaning toward the door and listening. He didn't hear anything. "Beth!"

"She's in there." Patsy Armstrong drew a key from her purse and opened the door. The room was dark, but Beth sat at her desk, which was right in front of a large, rectangular window. The door creaked shut behind him, and turning, Joel could make out Beth's bent head thanks to the streetlights across the street.

"It's not what you think," Patsy said.

"It's exactly what I think," Beth returned. "I saw you. You put the twenty Joel handed you in your pocket."

"I wasn't really going to steal the money," Patsy said. "I'd have given it back. I don't need the money. I just wanted…" Her words trailed off, and Joel wondered what she'd be saying if he weren't in the room.

"Me gone?"

"You gone," she agreed.

"What have I ever done to you?"

An oversized school clock suddenly developed a loud ticking sound that Joel hadn't noticed before. Without the kids, the room had an empty feeling.

After a minute, Patsy whispered, "It's your fault, all your fault. If you hadn't left that night, if I hadn't overheard you talking to your friend Max about taking off, running away, I'd have never…" Patsy's knees gave a little. She shifted forward, putting both hands on Beth's desk. "Honey, I promise you, we can make this right."

"What do you mean," Beth said cautiously, "about the night Joel left?"

Joel saw the exact moment that Patsy realized her error, and now there was no turning back.

"The night Joel left," Beth repeated, her words tight and strained.

For several moments, Patsy didn't say a word, just stood in front of Beth's desk as if she were a student about to be expelled.

Or worse.

"I did it for you," she finally said. "I needed the money to send you girls to college."

"Mom, what are you telling me?"

"I had to make sure you, at least, had a career that was stable, that would keep you safe if something happened down the line and I wasn't here."

Joel heard the steel in Patsy's voice. She'd do the same again if need be. He also heard the break in Beth's voice. "Mom, you took the Rodeo Club money? You framed Joel?"

"Look at you." Patsy sounded like a politician. "You have a degree, a well-paying job and if you're sensible about who you marry, you'll never have to worry. I did that for you. Because I love you. So you'd be safe."

"I'll shoulder the blame," Joel stated.

Beth wasn't listening. She stared at her mother, aghast. "You put me through college using stolen money?"

"If your father had lived, there'd have been enough. Raising three girls by myself, there was never enough. Never enough. Even when Linda didn't use the money I put aside, there wasn't enough. I started Susan in college, then she dropped out. I still owed money on her student loans by the time it was your turn. Can you believe that? But I wasn't letting you drop out. I knew you were going to college, and I would need the money when the time came."

"Beth," Joel began, "this isn't the best place or time. We can meet with the preacher, talk—"

"Did you regret your actions, Mom? Ever? Because I've only known about this for six seconds and I can't begin to tell you the regret I feel. And here's the truth. I have a degree in a field I wouldn't have chosen without your insistence. I wanted to go to art school."

"No guarantee of a job."

"Or at least be an art teacher."

"The first to be cut," Patsy reasoned.

"But it's what I love."

Behind them, the door opened and Billy came in. He turned on the light. Behind him, Matt peeked in. Patsy looked like a deer caught in the headlights, and Beth...

Beth was standing, strong and determined, and obviously not caring who heard her words. "Not the only thing I love." She looked right at Joel.

"Baby," Patsy said. "You need to think about—"

"I need to think about the freedom you just handed me." Beth came around the desk, her chin held high, and faced Joel. "How long have you known, Joel, that Mom took the money?"

"A little over a week."

"And why didn't you tell me?"

"I didn't want to hurt you."

She ignored her mother, probably not an easy thing to do, but she actually put her palm against Joel's chest. For a moment, he almost believed the gesture was one of gratitude. Then, she pushed him, hard enough so he'd know exactly what she was doing, and she said, "You've just become another person I love who's trying to keep me safe by forcing me to live a lie."

The amazing and surprising thing about Beth Armstrong, Joel decided a few minutes later, was her resilience.

She marched from the room. He felt like Silly Putty and wasn't sure his legs would take him out of the room. Right now, he'd put her on a bull. She had been repressed for so long and was just now showing her true colors.

He swallowed back all the things he wanted to do, wanted to say and gave Billy a helpless look.

"And the truth will set you free," Billy said.

Patsy gave a half snort, half sob.

"Come on, Patsy," Billy said, looking first at Joel and then at Matt. "Let's go to the school office, away from the tender hearts and tender ears. We need to put things to right."

"Uncle Joel, are you all right?"

Taking a deep breath, Joel stepped toward his nephew. "I will be, especially with your help."

"I'm a good helper," Matt said, and he took hold of Joel's hand.

As they walked down the hallway, all Joel could think about was how right Beth was. He hadn't trusted her to be strong enough to work alongside him. He hadn't trusted God enough to help them through a rough spot.

He found her, right where she belonged, back at face painting. In a daze, Joel went back to serving chili.

When Billy returned to the concession stand he told Joel, "Give her time."

"What are you doing with Patsy?"

"I've spoken to the principal, who called the school's attorney, and I'm sure he'll be calling us back come Monday. I called her son-in-law, Alex, and he's taking her to their house."

"House arrest," Joel tried to joke.

Billy didn't laugh.

The festival went on, most people blissfully unaware they'd missed a drama that had taken a cowboy to his knees.

As the crowd thinned and clean up began, a few people did come over, concern in their eyes and questions on their lips. Billy firmly stated, "This is a school matter and will be dealt with. I'm sure there will be something to report next week."

Joel wished it were already next week and he'd already managed to beg Beth's forgiveness.

Across the room, she finished a few last-minute faces. No doubt the kids would sleep with the design she'd painted on their faces. Suddenly, Joel couldn't help smiling. Back there, in her kindergarten classroom, Beth had gone through all the trauma with her mother, and with him, dressed like a French painter and sporting a fake mustache.

Now, that was a woman.

Caleb slept. Matt sat at a picnic table, an uneaten brownie in front of him. He'd spent the last few hours helping with concessions.

Joel took him a glass of milk.

"Will everything be all right?" Matt asked. Joel patted him on the shoulder. Poor kid. He didn't understand what he'd overheard, but he knew enough to be upset about it.

"Eventually everything will work out." A cop-out answer, one Joel had hated receiving when he was a kid. But he didn't have a better response.

"You still leaving tonight, Uncle Joel?"

"Just as soon as I load the pretend bulls into the back of Max's truck."

Frank Peabody plopped a wet rag on the table and started wiping. "I think I'd rather help with clean up over here. It'll be a lot quicker."

Any other time, Joel would have stayed to help with concession clean up, too, but tonight, he wanted to be on the road. He wanted to be going somewhere.

"I'm surprised you're leaving now," Frank said.

"There's a rodeo after Thanksgiving going on in Mesquite, Texas, if the weather allows. It'd get me back on the bull. I'm thinking it would be a good trial run. See if the circuit's still what I want to do."

"You coming back?" Frank asked.

"Absolutely."

His bags were in the truck bed, and he didn't need a map for where he was going. He'd been there a half-dozen times in the last eight years.

This was the first time his heart wasn't in it. Thirty minutes later, Joel left.

The late-night country radio station played a sad song. Joel turned it off. He didn't need to hear about someone else's woes.

Leaving without Beth and without the certainty that she'd be waiting was wrong. So wrong. When he hit the first Freeport 50 Miles sign, he thought about Jerry Tate. Keeping his word, Joel found Cathy Tate's number in his cell phone and called her, leaving a brief message on her answering machine. Joel's investigation wouldn't erase the kid's record, but now, at least, another kid wouldn't suffer the same fate thanks to Patsy Armstrong's manipulations.

Joel almost felt sorry for the woman. The interstate came into sight and Joel increased his speed a bit. Not that he was in a hurry. There were so many things he wanted to think about.

Thirty miles before the Freeport city limits, and because he wasn't paying attention, Joel hit a pothole big enough to swallow a cow.

He pulled off to the side of the road, got out and checked his tires. This wasn't going to work. His attention wasn't on the road. It was on a woman back in Roanoke.

Running away hadn't worked eight years ago. It wasn't working today, either.

God was on his side because his tires looked undamaged, and the road was clear. He could turn around and tell Beth how he felt. Stand beside her when she needed him most.

Climbing back behind the wheel, he started to close the door, but something stopped him—a small voice that wasn't in his head. The voice was attached to a head that was attached to a small hand that was pounding on the side of the truck.

"Why are we stopping? Did we have an accident?" Five-year-old Matt McCreedy, even in the cold November night, looked like he'd been having the time of his life hiding in the bed of his uncle's truck.

Joel deposited Matt in the passenger seat and gave a semi-serious scolding about the dangers of riding in a truck bed, then he took out his cell phone again. This time, he dialed his brother and let him know baby brother and middle son were coming home.

Matt had just given him one more reason.

Beth watched as Jared carried out the last of the trash bags. She was one of a handful of helpers still dealing with clean up as the clock ticked toward ten o'clock. Every time she turned around, either Jared or Billy or Mr. Peabody asked her to do something else. They were trying to keep her busy. But throughout all the menial tasks, all she felt was numb.

"I've got to get home," she finally told Jared. She was in the cafeteria's kitchen, standing amid the leaning towers of paper plates and cups that she'd helped put away.

This time, he didn't mention all the leftover plastic

silverware or bags of napkins that still needing gathering up. His attention was elsewhere, and instead of telling her to go ahead and go home, he stepped around her and said, "Thanks for coming back."

"I can't believe he hid in the back of my truck." Joel's voice echoed in the almost empty kitchen. Beth slowly pivoted.

"I wanted to go with you," Matt said sleepily. "I'd be good."

"I'd already turned around," Joel said. He wasn't looking at Matt or Jared, he was looking at her. "I'd forgotten something."

Jared backed out of the kitchen, dragging Matt with him, and whispering an excuse that sounded like "it's past our bedtime."

"What did you forget?" Beth asked. Her words were a little more clipped than they needed to be, but she wasn't about to make this easy for him. Tonight her world had exploded and she felt like she was standing on shifting sand and losing her footing.

"I forgot to tell you that I love you."

Words she had dreamed of hearing, but not tonight, not in a kitchen surrounded by paper goods and with the aroma of overcooked hot dogs. Not with the memory of her mother's misdeeds still echoing in her thoughts.

She nodded, but didn't tell him that she loved him.

He stayed where he was, hands down to his side, and a look in his eyes—his usually mischievous eyes—that she'd never seen before.

"I left for eight years," he said, telling her something she already knew. He left people. "There's a hole in my life that's waiting to be filled, and I'm smart enough now to realize it."

She understood about holes. One had just opened up right under her.

"I'm not leaving again. Not until I either have you beside me or waiting for me. I made a mistake in not telling you, but honestly, Beth, I was floored when I found out your mother had taken the money."

She nodded, but still didn't tell him that she loved him.

"I've never really felt like I was someone people needed, not my family, at least not all those years ago, and certainly not a few months ago. Now I realize the reason I didn't feel needed was because I didn't know how to give. In some ways, I only knew how to take. Plus, I always tried to do everything myself."

Her throat was starting to hurt.

"I was miserable."

She nodded, thinking that right now she *really* understood miserable. And, yes, how miserable her mother must be feeling about now. Her mother always tried to do everything herself, tried to make everything *right* for her girls. Slowly, the pressure on her heart lessened, especially when Joel said, "I need you."

And she certainly needed him. She didn't nod, didn't say the words, instead she went into his arms and held on, feeling his strength, his warmth, his love. He put a cold, rough hand on each side of her face and guided her lips to his. Never had a kiss felt so binding.

"Ahem," came a voice behind them.

Billy came in, looking both embarrassed and concerned. "Ah, the minivan's gone. Jared and the boys left. I think they forgot me."

It was exactly what the moment needed. Beth felt a giggle bubbling up. Chances were, in the next few months, there'd be some major upheavals among the Armstrong women, but Beth was strong enough to weather the storm. She, along with Joel—who would not be taking the blame—would stand beside her mother.

"I'll take you home in just a minute," Joel said. "I think you cut our kiss short."

Billy shook his head. "I don't think so."

Beth looked at Joel, and this time she laughed as she touched her upper lip. "He's right. If you kiss me any longer you're going to have quite a job getting rid of the mustache I just gave you."

"Paint?" he asked, squinting at what was left of her French mustache.

"Just a little smeary," she agreed.

"Do you like me with a mustache?"

"I love you with a mustache."

"And when the mustache turns gray?"

"I'll love you all the same."

Billy obviously couldn't take anymore. "I'll wait by the front door."

His stepfather hadn't made it out of the kitchen before Joel dipped his head again and tucked Beth tightly against him. "I'm home," he whispered, "when I'm with you."

Beth took his hand in hers. "Me, too."

At the kitchen door, Billy paused and said, *"You thrill me, Lord, with all You have done for me! I sing for joy because of what You have done."*

Finally, he left.

"How does Billy know exactly what I'm feeling right now?" Joel asked.

"It's not Billy," Beth said huskily. "That's God, written by David in Psalms."

"Then I thank God for putting His words to what I'm going to feel forever."

Beth knew that with Joel by her side, she'd be saying "I do" and "Me, too" for the rest of her life.

* * * * *

Dear Reader,

The idea for *Once Upon a Cowboy* came to me during a church service. No, really, I was paying attention to the sermon about the prodigal son. It's just that the minister was touching on some points I'd never really considered. First was the real definition of prodigal. It means heavy spending. For years, I thought it meant absent. Then, the lesson veered toward what the father could have done from the beginning, when his son asked for the inheritance early. The father could have taken his son to the city gate and had him stoned for being disobedient.

When I think about how many times I've been disobedient...

And, if you want to know the truth, I always pay attention to Prodigal Son sermons because I've never quite been able to shake the belief that the older son had something to complain about.

Thus, *Once Upon a Cowboy* was born, with a returning hero (Joel) who missed out in so many family memories but is soon determined not to miss out on any more—especially when he falls in love with a most unlikely heroine. Then, there's the heroine (Beth) who has to learn that taking risks is part of life—and who better to teach her than a wounded cowboy who wants to get in the saddle again? Throw in an older brother who needs his younger brother more than he'll admit, a trio of nephews who do not understand the concept of privacy, a stepfather who only wants what's best for both his boys, and a misguided mother who needs forgiveness, and you have the kind of story that only happily-ever-after can provide.

Thank you so much for reading *Once Upon a Cowboy*.

Pamela Tracy

Questions for Discussion

1. Knowing that he might not be welcomed, Joel heads for home. Why does he still think of it as home? What is he "really" hoping for? Did he return home for the right reason(s)?

2. Jared was more or less forced into taking in his young brother. What lessons does Jared learn from the fifth chapter of First Timothy: *anyone who does not provide for their relatives, and especially for their own household, has denied the faith and is worse than an unbeliever.* Have you ever had to learn this same lesson? How did it change you?

3. Matt is the nephew struggling the most with his mother's death. Why do you think this is? What does he need from Jared, Billy and Beth? What did Joel offer that the other three did not? What finally helps Matt overcome his pain?

4. Beth's mother played a key role in shaping her daughters' lives. More than her older siblings, Beth learned to play it safe. Why did her mother so fear the future? What could have changed the way Beth's mother dealt with her daughters? In what ways can you empathize with Patsy? If you had the chance to give her advice,

how would you word your advice so she might "really" listen?

5. Beth goes back and forth when it comes to giving Joel a chance. She blames a lot of her attitude on the fact that Joel leaves. Is this the real reason? What finally gets her to realize that he might be the man for her? How did this realization make her a stronger person?

6. Joel sets out to prove his innocence concerning the theft he's accused of. Why did it matter? Was it because he didn't want his reputation to be tarnished? Did he believe that maybe if he were proven innocent, Patsy would give him her blessing when it came to dating Beth? Or was there another reason?

7. Why did Billy feel the need to leave? Then, after Billy leaves, how does Jared's role change? How did these changes benefit Ryan, Matt and Caleb? Give one example for each of the boys.

8. Near the end of the book, Jared shares with Joel how he, too, wanted to run away but didn't. Name a time when you wanted to run away. What prevented you from doing it? How did you grow because you didn't run away?

9. When Beth's mother turns up guilty of taking the Rodeo Club money, she says she did it because

she only wanted to make sure her daughters had what they needed, in this case, an education. Is there anyone in the Bible who behaved as Patsy did? What kind of forgiveness does she deserve? From Beth? From Joel? From the school? In your own life, who do you need to forgive? And what do you need forgiven?

10. Joel had already decided to turn the truck around when he finds Matt in the truck bed because he realized what and where *home* was. Briefly describe what it is about your earthly dwelling that makes it home. Now, think about your heavenly home. How do you imagine it?

LARGER-PRINT BOOKS!

**GET 2 FREE
LARGER-PRINT NOVELS
PLUS 2 FREE
MYSTERY GIFTS**

Love Inspired®

SUSPENSE

RIVETING INSPIRATIONAL ROMANCE

Larger-print novels are now available...

YES! Please send me 2 FREE LARGER-PRINT Love Inspired® Suspense novels and my 2 FREE mystery gifts (gifts are worth about $10). After receiving them, if I don't wish to receive any more books, I can return the shipping statement marked "cancel". If I don't cancel, I will receive 4 brand-new novels every month and be billed just $4.99 per book in the U.S. or $5.49 per book in Canada. That's a saving of at least 23% off the cover price. It's quite a bargain! Shipping and handling is just 50¢ per book in the U.S. and 75¢ per book in Canada.* I understand that accepting the 2 free books and gifts places me under no obligation to buy anything. I can always return a shipment and cancel at any time. Even if I never buy another book, the two free books and gifts are mine to keep forever.

110/310 IDN FEH3

Name	(PLEASE PRINT)	

Address		Apt. #

City	State/Prov.	Zip/Postal Code

Signature (if under 18, a parent or guardian must sign)

Mail to the **Reader Service**:
IN U.S.A.: P.O. Box 1867, Buffalo, NY 14240-1867
IN CANADA: P.O. Box 609, Fort Erie, Ontario L2A 5X3

Not valid for current subscribers to Love Inspired Suspense larger-print books.

**Are you a current subscriber to Love Inspired Suspense books
and want to receive the larger-print edition?
Call 1-800-873-8635 or visit www.ReaderService.com.**

* Terms and prices subject to change without notice. Prices do not include applicable taxes. Sales tax applicable in N.Y. Canadian residents will be charged applicable taxes. Offer not valid in Quebec. This offer is limited to one order per household. All orders subject to credit approval. Credit or debit balances in a customer's account(s) may be offset by any other outstanding balance owed by or to the customer. Please allow 4 to 6 weeks for delivery. Offer available while quantities last.

Your Privacy—The Reader Service is committed to protecting your privacy. Our Privacy Policy is available online at www.ReaderService.com or upon request from the Reader Service.

We make a portion of our mailing list available to reputable third parties that offer products we believe may interest you. If you prefer that we not exchange your name with third parties, or if you wish to clarify or modify your communication preferences, please visit us at www.ReaderService.com/consumerschoice or write to us at Reader Service Preference Service, P.O. Box 9062, Buffalo, NY 14269. Include your complete name and address.

LISUSLP11B

LARGER-PRINT BOOKS!

**GET 2 FREE
LARGER-PRINT NOVELS
PLUS 2 FREE
MYSTERY GIFTS**

Love Inspired

Larger-print novels are now available...